CINDERELLA'S LEGACY

SHONNA SLAYTON

AMARETTO PRESS

To the fans of Cinderella's Dress
who wanted to know more.

FOREWORD

This tale is a companion novella to *Cinderella's Dress* and *Cinderella's Shoes*. Readers wanted to know more about the backstory, and I was happy to oblige. It was pure fun to imagine Cinderella as a real girl from the highland region of what is now modern-day Poland.

While *Cinderella's Dress* and *Cinderella's Shoes* remain as true to real 1940s history as I could make a fairy tale, this novella, *Cinderella's Legacy*, is a mishmash of elements taken in reverse from the original novels. Set in some unknown distant past, you won't find any of these events on a timeline, but I do pull several elements of Poland's rich cultural history into the story. I hope you enjoy reading it, and if you wonder if something is real, it might be. You can look it up or check out my website for more.

It was tricky business to decide what to call this Cinderella. The Polish name for Cinderella is Kopciuszek, but given that the story takes place in the land that would become Poland, all the dialogue is "translated" into English, which puts us right back at using Cinderella. However, she wasn't born with the name Cinderella, so I chose a name from the region that contained elements similar to Cinderella—Petronela.

PROLOGUE

*E*smerelda lazed in bed and waved her hand to start the kettle for tea. Tiny sparkles floated through the air and swirled around the fire as it flickered to life. She congratulated herself for her cleverness in filling the kettle with water the night before, so she didn't have to get up to go to the well.

She was not as young as she used to be and enjoyed a good sleeping-in, especially on a cold spring morning. She burrowed under her quilt a bit longer as the starlings chatted amongst themselves with happy songs. An off note sounded and Esmerelda winced.

Poor bird, with a voice like that it won't find a mate.

Again, the off note, only louder and sounding more like a human noise. Esmerelda cocked her head. That wasn't a bird; it was a baby's cry.

She rolled out of bed, her warm feet hitting the cold plank floor. She shuffled around, looking for her slippers before throwing open the door.

A simple straw basket had been left at her doorstep and deep inside wiggled a newborn babe. Days old if it were a week.

"Oh, my." She peered down close.

It momentarily paused its fussing, but its face remained screwed up, lips trembling like it was about to deliver a repeat performance.

Esmerelda scanned the meadow and then the path into the forest. A black bear ambled by, unperturbed by any strangers who might be lurking in the woods and watching to see what she would do with the baby.

She *tsked* before picking up the infant. *Those villagers throw rotten vegetables at me one day and leave me a baby the next. Wish they'd make up their minds.*

"But you, sweet thing, know nothing of that. Not yet." She cuddled the infant, breathing in the innocent baby smell.

After bringing the child into the cottage, she set the basket close to the embers of the fireplace for inspection. It may be spring, but up in the mountains, the mornings were still nippy.

"What have we here?" She unwrapped the blanket. "A lass." After a quick nappy change and a thorough but fruitless search of the basket, Esmerelda tucked the infant back into her soft knitted blanket. The creature fussed and jerked her arms. Likely hungry.

Esmerelda placed her hands on her ample hips as she surveyed her home. The cottage was built for one. Esmerelda only. It held all her favorite and comfortable things. Her copper pots and pans, her small pantry, a window filled with herbs fighting each other for the sun. Her cozy bed—which she should still be curled up in, thank you very much, and—

Twill, twill, screeeech!

The kettle pushed out the steam with such force it could not be ignored. Much like the squalling infant who startled at the sound and cried along with it.

"All right, little one." She poured the water into the teapot and added a bundle of tea leaves and herbs. "You sit tight while I talk to Ania."

The old mother goat had what was likely her last kid three days ago and, being a sympathetic mother, would be willing to share her milk with the babe.

Keeping one eye on the forest, Esmerelda set to work milking the goat. A rustle of leaves in the lilac bush near the garden caught her attention. She shifted her seat to face the bush. "Found a wee babe this morn, I did," she said nice and loud. "Looks good and strong. Well, its lungs are at any rate. A fine young thing who needs its mama." She shifted again on the stool. Her old bones weren't what they used to be.

"Such a pretty thing. Big long eyelashes. Wide innocent eyes. It deserves to be loved, it does. Not aban—" she stopped herself. She had no idea what the mother was going through. "Life is precious. A child ought to know its mama. And her mama ought to know her."

Esmerelda's pointed words seemed to have no effect on the mother hidden in the forest, if that's who was making the bushes rustle. She couldn't tell from here. Perhaps it was the father, or a sibling.

"Hungry thing, isn't she? I can hear the bawling from here. But once she's fed, she'll quiet down. They're not so much trouble as they grow and settle into our world. We get used to them. Find we adjust to one another just fine."

She stood and put her hands on her hips. No response. Esmerelda thought about making a sudden run for where she thought the mother stood but knew she would be easily outrun. No sense in frightening the watcher away for certain.

"I was planning on going away for the summer. If'n you want the wee thing back, you can come collect her in a few days, a week or two. But don't wait too long or you'll lose the chance."

She thought then that she heard a sob but couldn't be sure. You had to give them a timeline so they'd think about it. If Esmerelda were saddled with a babe, she wouldn't be going away for the summer anyway. Best to stay put in case the someone changed her mind. A fairy godmother wasn't supposed to do the raising, only the helping.

CHAPTER 1

*P*etronela lay in bed listening to her father getting ready to leave: the clank of his armor as he fitted on his arm guards; the high-pitched swish when he sheathed his sword; the rustle of his travel pack as he stuffed it with provisions.

Last night they sat together at dinner eating *makowiec*, her special dessert, and he didn't tell her he was going. Ever since Mama died, he hadn't the heart to tell her bad news, so he acted like nothing bad *ever* happened. As if not talking about it made it not real.

When he was home, they only spoke of happy things. Butterflies in the meadow. The newly hatched chicks in the barn. Petronela learning a fancy new sewing stitch. It almost made things worse, since they couldn't talk about their sadness.

Papa's clunky mountain boots clomped down the hall, but grew quieter near her room. The squeak of the door betrayed him as he entered. He was coming in to say goodbye.

She snapped her eyes shut, playing his game. She'd pretend she was asleep and let him slip out thinking he had spared her another sad goodbye. The servants would tell her at dinner and then spoil her with sweets and attention until he returned from battle.

He stood over her for a painfully long time. Her eyelids fluttered as she almost gave in and peeked.

"Goodbye, Petronela, love," he whispered.

She remained unmoving, not even breathing. *My name means rock.*

When he finally left, she felt the tickle of a feather land on her arm, fallen from his armor.

The hussars had the best-looking armor of all the armies with wings made of large feathers mounted on their backs. The wings were supposed to symbolize the eagle, but all the children knew they were angel wings, and that under their protection, nothing would happen to the kingdom. When the men rushed into battle the wind made the feathers clatter together in an awesome noise that petrified the enemy.

The hussars and the beautiful castle watched over the town.

Rising out of the granite mountain, the castle appeared as if it grew there on its own. Only the beloved king and queen and their surviving prince lived in residence, the oldest prince having died in an avalanche one terribly horrible winter. In the shadow of the castle, Petronela could not be afraid, no matter how badly the stable hands or boys in the village tried to scare her.

She snatched the feather and pulled it under the cover before Papa could look back and notice it lying there. He wouldn't want her to know he was going off to battle. He turned at the door and gave her one last look. He always did, and if he noticed her squinting through her lashes, he never let on.

Sometime later, the maid woke her with a special treat—breakfast in bed. Petronela would have enjoyed it immensely if it were not for the sad eyes with which Filomena watched her.

"Eat with me," Petronela said.

Filomena tilted her head. "You know the master doesn't like that. I ate with the others early this morning in the kitchen."

"How long will he be gone this time?" She and Filomena had an understanding. Petronela would do as she was told—as much as she could—and Filomena wouldn't talk to her like she was a child.

"Long. He wants me to take you to your aunt's house so you'll have your cousins to play with." She quirked her mouth.

Neither of them liked her cousins.

"Can't I stay here with you?" She put on her best sad face. The sad face worked really well when she was little, but now that she was "growing into a young lady" it worked less frequently.

"Afraid not, miss. Your aunt is expecting you." Her look softened and grew conspiratorial. "But we don't have to leave right way. She doesn't know *when* to expect you."

Petronela grinned. She finished her breakfast with renewed gusto so she could get on with the day, now that she knew it would be a fun one. With father gone, she could play with the servants all she liked and not have to visit with her horrid cousins.

After breakfast was done, she dashed outside to play. Passing by the stables, she called out to the stable boy.

"Aron, I'm going to the creek."

"Morning, Petronela. Are you setting up for the fairies again?"

"Yes, I have to make them an extra special place this time because I'm forced to go stay with my cousins while Papa is gone."

"Sorry."

"Me, too. Find me when you're finished with your chores."

Midmorning, Aron joined her in the ravine where she was almost finished building a fairy garden. She had found an especially soft patch of moss near a rivulet of melting snow trickling down from the mountain. Using twigs and tall grass, she'd fashioned a tiny gazebo by the water.

Seeing her friend coming, she tucked her mussed hair behind her ear. She'd gotten it caught in a tree when she'd climbed up to get a closer look at a bird's nest filled with chirping babies.

"Nela, you're too old to believe in fairies," Aron said, bending down to look at the gazebo.

Petronela continued her work. "I want to make sure they don't forget about me."

"It won't be that long, will it?"

"Don't know. Papa's never sent me away before."

"Well, don't worry about your animals, I'll take good care of them."

"I know you will, Aron." Aron was the closest thing she had to a brother. His parents worked on the estate, so they'd practically grown up together.

The dinner bell clanged, calling Petronela in. "It's not time to eat yet," she said with a frown. "Maybe Papa left me a surprise. Race you!"

Running and laughing, she sped to the house. She arrived first and bounded up the porch before bursting through the door. "I win!" she called, looking over her shoulder and running smack into the stiff form of her aunt.

Petronela gasped as a coldness traveled through her veins all the way to her fingertips, turning her hands to ice.

"Back straight. Chin up," her aunt said. "Your mother would be ashamed if she knew how wild her child has become since her death." She picked a twig out of Petronela's hair. "I had no idea how bad things had gotten here."

She kissed Petronela first on one cheek, then the other, and back to the first. Then she sent a cool look in the maid's direction. "Where are her bags? I haven't got all day."

Her aunt stood tall, stretched tight enough she might snap at any moment. Her hair was pulled back in a severe updo and tucked into an outrageously flowered hat. She wore her very best dress, white with red poppies; it almost looked like the traditional wedding dress of the highlands.

Petronela had lost her voice. "I-I" she stammered, looking to the maid for help.

"We're almost ready," Filomena said. "Won't be much longer now."

"Well then? Off with you." Aunt Marzena clapped twice in dismissal.

The maid smiled an apology to Petronela while curtsying to the aunt. Petronela followed after the maid, but her aunt called her back, pinning her with her dark eyes.

"There'll be no nonsense at my home. You will act properly and obey instruction. You are obviously lacking a woman's direction. My daughters will be excellent examples for you. We'll have you turned around in no time. Your father won't even recognize you when he returns."

Petronela stood gaping. "Papa likes me the way I am." For that matter, so did she. She wouldn't be turned into a mini version of one of her cousins.

"Enough. There will be no talking back."

"Papa's groomsmen were going to bring me to your place later this week," Petronela said in a futile attempt at putting off the inevitable.

"I had business to attend in town, so you can come with me now."

Aunt Marzena walked around the room, touching a painting here, pressing a cushion there. "I'll leave my buggy in your stables and we'll take the coach. There'll be more room."

Petronela tried to think of another excuse to delay the trip, but the shock of it all had dulled her brain.

All too soon, her trunks were packed and the servants began loading them into Father's best coach, the fancy one trimmed in gold that he bought for Mama for their first wedding anniversary. Aunt Marzena had always hated that coach, so it was an odd choice for her to take to her cottage.

Petronela waved goodbye to the stained-glass window above

the door depicting a majestic oak tree, a ritual she'd developed after her mother died. Father said oak trees had always been Mother's favorite, so that's why they'd chosen to make that particular scene.

Remembering the feather, Petronela ran back upstairs. She stopped short at the top of the landing. The door to her mother's room was open, which was curious because Father liked it to stay closed. He went in late at night sometimes and stayed for hours. She, herself, liked to go in and play whenever father was gone. Mama's perfume, a sweet blend of the garden flowers was already starting to fade. Maybe that was why Father insisted they keep the door closed. So Mama's smell wouldn't go away.

Aunt Marzena stood inside.

"What are you doing in here?" Petronela said, a pit forming in her stomach. "Father won't like it."

"She was my sister," said Aunt Marzena. "I miss her, too."

But the way Aunt Marzena sized up the room like she was taking inventory didn't look like she was missing her sister. It looked like she was making plans.

CHAPTER 2

*L*ittle Nadzia stole a peek at Esmerelda and adjusted her gait to match, taking small steps and not skipping. She held her head high and looked forward instead of investigating all the new sights they passed by. But a few steps later, she'd forgotten herself and raced ahead, trying to see the next thing beyond the bend in the road.

Esmerelda's heart squeezed. She'd never expected to care this way for a human child. Of all the girls she'd helped over the years, it was always a job.

Find the girl, figure out her problem, help her to solve it.

Of course, she cared what happened to these other girls, but this. *This.*

As a baby, Nadzia would sleep swaddled with one hand tucked up against her ear as if listening to a far-off song, and her long eyelashes lay as bird's wings against her rosy cheeks. Esmerelda had never seen anything so beautiful.

She'd watched the child grow from a wee babe into a bubbly, excited little girl interested in everything in their valley. Together, they explored the forest, the creeks, and planted the garden.

Esmerelda had thought she liked being alone—preferred it—but that was only because she was used to it. Now, she was used to this little girl who didn't belong with a fairy godmother.

Today was Nadzia's first trip into town. They were going to buy ribbons for her hair, and the girl couldn't bottle the excitement.

"Babuszka, tell me again about the ribbons."

Esmerelda smiled gently, wondering how long the girl's excitement would last if the real purpose of their trip were made known. "Silk ribbons, long enough to braid into your hair. In colors of the rainbow. Reds and blues and violets and yellows."

The girl spun with her arms up, pleased with the answer.

They were closer to town now, so Esmerelda took a moment to retie her own kerchief so it cast her face in shadow. She wasn't in the mood for the people's nonsense today, so the less she saw of them, the better.

Her mission was to find one young woman only. The one who stared at her longer than the rest. Who, instead of calling insults, or running away, drank in the sight of the small child at her side.

At six years old, Nadzia had grown into a bright young thing, and Esmerelda didn't know how she was going to let her go. But, it was past time. The child was never hers to keep.

Surely the mother would be in different circumstances now and ready to take her. Esmerelda had stayed in the mountains all these years, but her itching feet wanted her to move on, and she had been neglecting her duties.

However, it didn't feel right to take the child away without giving the mother another chance.

"How will I know which one to buy?" Nadzia asked.

"We'll know it when we see it. Be attentive, like when you're in the forest searching for mushrooms. You've got to find the kind that's good, not poisonous."

Laughter spilled from the child. "But Babuszka, ribbons are ribbons. How can one be good and one be poisonous?"

"True, ribbons are ribbons. You find the one you like. I'll keep a watch for the poison."

At the sight of all the buildings, Nadzia stopped and stared in wonder.

"Like our cottage, only bigger and more of them," Esmerelda said.

"No, it's not that." Nadzia pointed beyond the houses to the massive building up on the mountain.

"The castle? But we can see that from our valley."

"But it's so close here. Can we go there after I get my ribbons?"

"No, dearie. That's where the king lives. You need an invitation to go there."

"It's so beautiful, Babuszka."

Esmerelda held the girl's hand as they turned the corner into the main marketplace. The missing mother was likely to pass through the area at some point during the day. The stalls were in a bustle as shopkeepers bargained with shoppers.

Nadzia tugged on her hand, eager to get moving. "Look at all the people. I didn't know there were this many in the whole world."

"There's no hurry. We're going to spend the day here."

Cautiously, Esmerelda led the girl systematically past the egg sellers and the chandlers and the bakers, only making eye contact with women of birthing age.

Meanwhile, Nadzia drank in the sights, inhaled the cinnamon and tallow scents. A look of rapture spread across her countenance. "Look, there's a child like me." She pointed at a small boy herding two ducks.

At the basket seller, Esmerelda's kerchief slipped, and the man recognized her.

He sneered. "You're not welcome in town."

His wife looked up from her work to see what the fuss was about. "Go back to the mountains where you belong," she added.

Esmerelda continued her quest, hoping Nadzia hadn't heard.

"Why did they say such things to us?" asked Nadzia.

"Some don't know any better, and those that do choose to be mean."

"I don't like it," said Nadzia. "They need someone to teach them to talk right."

"Yes, they do, dearie. But it won't be me right now. We've got shopping to do." Esmerelda continued her slow, methodical visit to every stall.

While Nadzia shopped for ribbons, Esmerelda shopped for a mother. She'd seen plenty of surreptitious glances, but not one with a desperate, curious look. There was still time.

"How about one of these?" Esmerelda asked. They stood at a fabric stall where a tree made of dowels created a lovely display of ribbons in shades of blue and green and orange.

Nadzia fingered them, one at a time.

"Well?"

"The feel is not quite right," she said earnestly. "I'm to wait until I find the one meant for me."

Esmerelda was tempted to chide her and then make her choose one, but she understood how it was to be careful with a big decision. And for a child from the mountain on her first shopping trip, this was a big decision. Besides, she'd coached the girl to take her time so that Esmerelda could look for the mother. Neither one of them had found quite what they were looking for.

CHAPTER 3

*T*he coach made a slow procession through town. Aunt Marzena insisted on driving through the center of the market where all the people gathered, the velvet curtains pinned back so she could look out—or the townspeople could look in—Petronela wasn't sure which.

She, herself, shied away from the curious stares, not wanting her shame on display. A girl without a mother, a father off to battle, and having to rely on the goodness of her Aunt's heart to take her in. Or at least, that's how Aunt Marzena kept framing it.

"You should thank me I'm not leaving you all alone in that mansion. I don't know why my sister ever bought something so large when it was only the three of you. Such a waste. I at least, had two daughters to help fill a house."

Petronela didn't answer. She focused on the positives, like being allowed to bring her maid with her. The long stay might be bearable with a confidante nearby.

Filomena sat up with the coachman, no doubt fretting over how she would fit in with the other servants. In Father's home, all the servants were treated well and enjoyed a great deal of independence. Not so in Aunt Marzena's household. Those servants were wound up as tight as the grandfather clock in the foyer. Filomena would be just as miserable as she, but together they would endure until Papa came home.

"Halt!" Aunt Marzena called suddenly, tapping the roof with her parasol. The driver stopped in the middle of the road. "I see an old friend," she said. "I must speak with her at once. Driver?"

Aunt's coachman hopped down and opened the door for her. He set out the stool for her to step down and waited patiently, ignoring the protests of the people having to go around the coach blocking the road.

Petronela pressed herself into the padded cushion, trying to hide from her aunt's inconsiderate behavior. Everyone had to walk around them, and if there were any carriages behind them, well, they'd have to wait until her aunt was done with her visiting. If that's even what she was doing. She was probably creating a scene so everyone could see her in the grand carriage. Parked smack in the middle of town, it was hard to miss.

"Look!" cried a sweet voice outside the window. "There's a princess in there."

Petronela smiled. She wasn't a princess, though a country girl wouldn't know the difference, given the grand coach. She popped her head out the window to see who it was.

A little hand started to wave. There. A small thing with brown hair tied back in a messy braid. She was standing with an elderly woman who hid her face with a kerchief and wore the clothing of the mountain folk. Must be the girl's grandmother and, if Petronela guessed correctly, they were here on a rare trip to town.

Petronela waved back and the girl jumped up and down with excitement. Struck with an idea, she reached into one of the bags at her feet and pulled out a robin's egg blue ribbon. "Come here," she said, waving the girl over.

The girl broke away from her guardian who cried out and reached for her.

Petronela leaned over, dropping the ribbon into the girl's outstretched hand. "For you. Now, go back to your babuszka and be sure to hold her hand. We don't want her to get lost, do we?"

The girl shook her head solemnly, eyes wide as she grasped the treasure.

The grandmother caught up to the little girl and grasped her hand. Her kerchief slid back as she looked up into the carriage. A wizened face with graying hair and piercing eyes stared back at Petronela.

The old woman opened her mouth, but hesitated and cocked her head. Her eyes narrowed slightly. In recognition? Petronela had never seen the woman before in her life. Maybe the babuszka knew her mother once upon a time, and she was wondering what she should say.

"Thank you, miss," the babuszka said, her free hand reaching up and clasping the amber necklace at her throat. "We've come to market today for this very thing."

"Oh, how lovely," Petronela said. "Your granddaughter is very sweet. I hope she'll make good use out of the ribbon."

"Quit hanging out the window." Aunt Marzena spoke harshly as she climbed back into the carriage.

"Yes, ma'am." Petronela settled back into her seat, but not before she winked and waved at the little girl one last time before the coach pulled away.

"When we are out in public, you are to act with the utmost grace. Don't talk to strangers, especially the common folk of this town. Beggars, every last one of them. They didn't ask you for money, did they?"

"No, ma'am. No one asked me for money."

"Good. Your father arranged for me to manage your allowance while he is gone."

"But Filomena does that."

"Not anymore."

Petronela crossed her arms and stared out the window as they passed the chandler's, the cobbler's, and then the baker's shops. She couldn't believe her father would approve of such a change.

"Don't look glum. Your father has left instructions, so you'll be well cared for. He coddles you because he feels bad that you are without a mother. Something we hope to rectify soon."

The hairs on the back of Petronela's neck prickled. "What does that mean?"

Aunt Marzena didn't answer. Instead, she tapped the ceiling of the carriage with her parasol. The coachman stopped the vehicle in front of a toy shop.

"Your father has left you a present here. We're to pick it up now. Be sure to share with your cousins, yes? They have to work so hard for their belongings. It's different when a husband dies than when a wife dies."

Aunt Marzena had introduced so many conflicting thoughts in the last five minutes Petronela didn't know what to focus on first.

"Are you daft? Come on, child." Aunt Marzena marched into the store, jingling the bell on her way in.

Perplexed, Petronela scrambled after her.

"Miss Petronela, this way, please." An aproned shop girl led her to the back room where a miniature fairy landscape was set up. Tiny houses in the shape of acorns and mushrooms and miniature trees formed a village. Little ponds and flower bushes dotted the green hills. A small garden looked like it was growing tiny carrots and radishes.

"What is this?" she asked, picking up a fairy in a purple dress with iridescent wings.

"A gift from your father," the shop girl smiled. "He said you were to choose whatever you liked."

A feeling of warmth radiated through Petronela's heart. Maybe father did know the trial he was asking of her. Bless him. She could live peacefully with her cousins, if not happily, knowing that he loved her so.

"Hurry up," Aunt Marzena said, standing in the doorway. She looked down her nose at the fairy village.

Petronela scanned the village. How was she to choose? She wouldn't want to separate friends, or leave anyone out, feeling unwanted. The shop girl eagerly pointed out her favorites, but Aunt Marzena's snuffling and toe-tapping put pressure on her to make rash decisions.

She picked out a tree house and two fairies who looked like they were friends. A gazebo and a garden and a teapot and a tiny set of books.

"How many did he say I could choose?" she finally asked, looking longingly at an old gentlemanly fairy and another plump fairy holding a pie who looked like they went together.

"As many as you want."

She scooped up the new couple and found a house for them to live in and a little wheelbarrow to lean up against their house. Another fairy sitting off to the side alone, seemed to be trying to get her attention. "And who are you?" she asked, picking her up. She wore a blue dress like a lily and held a bemused smile like she was ready to share a secret.

"I think you have enough now, don't you?" Aunt Marzena said. She crossed her arms.

Petronela returned the fairy to her spot.

"That's all, thank you," she said to the shop girl. But she looked longingly at the little fairy in the blue dress. She should have chosen her first.

Aunt Marzena turned around and went back into the main part of the store. The shop girl winked and tucked the blue-clad fairy into the box with the others. Then she went around and quickly added several other pieces Petronela had examined.

"Your father told me to double what you asked for," she whispered.

"That's my papa." Petronela took out the blue-clad fairy so she could hold her the rest of the trip.

CHAPTER 4

*A*unt Marzena's house was a modest size, rising two stories and covered with ivy. A curved staircase connected the levels and at the base of this staircase, the cousins watched with interest behind their fans as trunk after trunk was unloaded and carted up to Petronela's room.

"Why does she have so much stuff?" asked the one called Hortensia hanging over the banister.

"She thinks she's a princess," said the other, Jolanta, sniffing. "Her father spoils her rotten." She adjusted her flower crown.

"She does carry airs."

They spoke as if Petronela couldn't hear them. Were they the ones who were daft? They couldn't be that rude. Maybe they were both simpletons like the baker's assistant in town. Perhaps kindness would win them over, and they would learn to get along.

"Hello, cousins," she said with as much cheer as she could muster. "Wait until you see what my father gave me. A fairy garden, ever so splendid. We can set it up in your playroom if you like, so we can all enjoy it."

Hortensia rolled her eyes and Jolanta laughed.

Petronela felt her smile slipping. "I'll go check on my room." She excused herself and followed the servants up the stairs. She'd endure for Papa's sake, and Mama's. They're Mama's kin and they should all try to get along. Mama did say she and her sister had their moments. In the end, they matured and got along. Although, Mama married young and moved away from her sister. Not living in the same house surely helped. But until she could go back home, Petronela would use every ounce of her patience to keep the waters calm. Staying here would make her father's return all the more sweet.

Petronela passed her aunt's room, the playroom, her cousins' bedrooms, and then found the guest room where she would be staying. As the guest room, it was the fanciest room after Aunt Marzena's. Painted a soft lavender with striped wallpaper, it held a four-poster bed with overstuffed mattress which aligned with the window so that Petronela would wake up looking out onto the flower garden below.

A maid in a navy-blue uniform and apron stood near the bed, working her way through Petronela's trunks.

"May I help?" Petronela asked.

"No, miss. Go outside and play. It's a lovely day."

"There's plenty of time for that. If we work together, we'll be done in no time." *And I'd rather be safely alone here, than risk running into my prickly cousins.*

"'Tis maid's work, miss. Your aunt won't like you helpin' out."

"What can she do? It's not like she can ask my father to come get me, although I would like her to do so."

"All right, miss. But don't go broadcasting I let you help."

"Our secret," Petronela said, snatching a pile of stockings from the maid's hands. There's one new friend, as long as they were not caught being friendly. Aunt Marzena kept a deeper separation between help and family in this household.

In no time, they were down to one last piece of luggage aside from the box of fairies near the door. Despite her cousins' lack of enthusiasm, Petronela would still lay out the new toys as a peace offering. Perhaps barriers would come down once they started to play together.

"What is this?" asked Jolanta, barging into the room. She bounded over and pulled out a square of fur.

"A muff," Petronela said, "to keep your hands warm when it turns cold. Do you like it?"

The girl started to nod, but after catching a look from her older sister standing in the doorway, shook her head.

Petronela frowned at the exchange. "You can have it." She hoped to be back home with father before she'd have use of it.

Jolanta held it to her chest, turning her back on her sister. "Thank you." She ran out of the room, presumably to her own bedroom to find a place for the new treasure.

"If you're finished here," Hortensia said to the maid, "there's a mess to clean up in my room." She didn't even look at Petronela before leaving again.

"Yes, miss." The maid dropped the last pair of shoes into the wardrobe and scurried out of the room.

In those few minutes, Petronela surmised the pecking order of the house. Aunt Marzena then Hortensia then Jolanta and, somewhere along with the maids, stood Petronela.

I may as well go and make acquaintance with the staff. This time of day most of them would be in the kitchen. Hortensia's irritated voice floated out of her bedroom as Petronela tip-toed down the hall to the stairs. Thankfully, Jolanta's door was closed, as was Aunt Marzena's, and the white carpet was thick and absorbed footsteps.

In fact, the entire house was eerily quiet, as if holding its breath, waiting for the next command to be voiced. At her house, the staff would be talking and joking, singing to make the day go by more pleasantly. Not here. The stark whites and blacks used in the decorations reflected the feel of the house. No warm wood paneling here. Not even a cozy library to curl up in and escape in a book.

Petronela found her own maid in the kitchen washing the dishes.

"What are you doing in here little miss?" Filomena paused to wipe the sweat off her forehead.

"Hoping to meet everyone." But none of the servants would make eye contact with her. "Seems like now is not a good time."

Filomena spun her around and marched her to the door amidst skeptical looks from the kitchen staff. "Get yourself upstairs and make friends with your cousins. Your mama would want you to."

"Can't I stay with you?" she asked. "I could help you with the bread like I do at home."

"I'm not makin' the bread. Over here I'm the low branch on the tree. I be doing the dishes and tending the fires. You'll get yourself all covered in the cinders if you help me. Now scoot."

CHAPTER 5

"Do you remember the princess we saw in town, Babuszka?"

Esmerelda nodded. The princess had become a frequent topic of discussion since their trip.

"The way she stopped to talk to me and give me one of her ribbons, she was ever so kind, just like in the stories you tell me." Nadzia gently stroked her new kitten, born while they had been in the village. They'd been constant companions these last few months. Nadzia had set up a little bed of blankets near the hearth and the mother cat had allowed the assistance. "I hope I can see the princess again."

"Maybe one day." Esmerelda tied a new batch of sage up in the rafters to dry. She was conflicted about what to do. They'd spent the entire day in town and hadn't found the mother. Perhaps she had moved away, or was a mountain girl herself.

They'd tried at the next town as well, but with the same result. The mother was gone. The third town over was too far for a new mother to walk just to leave her child with someone. It wouldn't make sense. The mother might live in the mountains, but if so, she'd have had plenty of opportunity to make up an excuse to visit the cottage to check on her little girl. But she hadn't.

Esmerelda wouldn't leave Nadzia with just anyone, nor could she take her traveling with her either. There were too many temptations for her to use her fairy magic on the road, and that would risk exposing who she was to the child. Nadzia couldn't know. At least not until she was old enough to keep her own counsel.

"Can we go back to town soon?" Nadzia asked. "I liked it. There were so many people. And children like me. I saw some shopping with their mothers in the market, and others were playing a game in the square."

Guilt flooded Esmerelda. She wasn't the proper kind of mother for this dear child who needed more companionship than the goats and the chickens. It wasn't Nadzia's fault that the townspeople didn't know what to do with Esmerelda. She'd tried to act more humanlike, but she was a fairy godmother and that wasn't something you told everyone. Not if you wanted to be left alone.

"Yes, I saw them, too. But you've played with the mountain children. I know how much little Stefa likes to see your animals. And the peddler sometimes brings his grandchildren with him."

Nadzia frowned, and Esmerelda could almost read her thoughts. It wasn't the same, playing with a child once every month or two, and sometimes not even that frequently. The animals were cuddly and sometimes funny, but they didn't talk back. And a girl needed to share her secret thoughts and be rewarded with someone else's dreams in return.

"If you want, we can take more trips to town. We can sell our herbs at the monthly market and then you could talk to the other children helping their parents."

Nadzia's face lit up. "Could we go twice each month? They have a market every week."

"The monthly market is plenty frequent for us. It's a long way to walk, and that's when the other mountain families attend. You'll feel more welcome."

Nadzia cocked her head, as if the thought hadn't even crossed her mind that she wouldn't be welcomed. Esmerelda searched for a way to steer the conversation another direction. It was she, the fairy godmother, who wasn't welcomed in town. She shouldn't project her problems onto the innocent.

"What I mean is you'll meet children who live closer to us."

Esmerelda's words had no effect. The child's features continued to look bothered.

"Listen," Nadzia said, a slow smile spreading across her face. "The winged men are flying home." She ran out the door before Esmerelda could stop her.

What Nadzia had heard was the clacking of wings coming from a man spurring his horse to the front of the slow-moving line. His feathers were white, and he was replacing another white-winged warrior.

The other warriors rode in pairs where they could on the narrow mountain path. Their gray wings and armor plates coupled with their red uniforms made for a handsome, stately lot.

The other winged warriors were silent but for the shifting of leather and clanking of armor, tall in their saddles.

Not many carried their long lances, meaning they had been used and broken in battle. Those who did, carried them attached to their saddles, the white and red banners waving like undulating grass, not flying straight in the wind as they did when the horses ran in battle.

The return ride was not as resplendent as when she and Nadzia saw them leave the valley. Nor were the men riding relaxed and happy, like when a war was over. No, these soldiers were still very much in military mode. This march home was merely a lull. A change in direction.

To Nadzia, it must look like a parade. Sunlight glinted off

their silver armor like flashing lights, and the leopard pelts slung across their shoulders were worn proudly, as in a hunting victory. Nadzia grinned and waved both hands high above her head.

Some of the winged warriors waved back, rewarding her enthusiasm.

What Nadzia wasn't old enough to understand was that until recently, their small kingdom had been protected by these tall, rugged mountains. That was, until the kingdom on the other side of the mountain began taking aggressive action to move the boundaries, ultimately wanting to absorb the entire mountain range and valleys into their own. The mountain people were a proud people and wouldn't acquiesce.

Esmerelda frowned as the last man was swallowed up in the forest. "Nadzia, let's harvest the garden today. We'll start our canning early this year."

It wouldn't hurt for them to be prepared for the worst.

CHAPTER 6

When Petronela woke, she could tell something exciting was going on in the house. If it were early spring, she'd think it was spring cleaning, but given the lateness of the calendar, she supposed the maids running around throwing windows open and batting rugs outside signaled a household getting ready for an important guest.

At least if they were having company, Hortensia and Jolanta should be on their best behavior.

Petronela padded around in her nightshirt until she found a maid polishing the silver. "Excuse me, what's going on?"

The maid answered by pointing in the direction of the kitchen.

Petronela skirted past another maid dashing by with an armful of bedding to the washing room. The sound of clanging pots spilled into the hallway long before she got to the kitchen. The place was all abuzz with two additional chefs brought in from town chopping carrots and cabbage, dressing roasts with rosemary, and mixing puddings.

Petronela's own maid was arm-deep in soapy water washing dishes.

"What's happening?" Petronela asked her.

"The men have been called in and transferred around the other side of the mountain. Your father will be here for one day. Let's make it a good one. No need to trouble him with your worries. When he's home for good we'll tell him everything, okay? Your aunt might think those girls are perfect angels, but your father will see through. He's a sharp man."

"Papa! Oh, that's the best surprise. How may I help?"

"Off you go and get ready. Just stay away from your cousins so they can't spoil your joy."

Petronela nodded. She'd confided in Filomena what the cousins had been up to since she'd arrived. For the most part, Hortensia had vacillated between ignoring and insulting her, but Jolanta had taken to stealing her things one by one.

Perhaps when she gave her the muff that first day Jolanta took it as a sign that she could have all of Petronela's belongings. But when Petronela accused her of stealing the fairy pieces, she denied she'd taken anything.

Once Jolanta had started stealing pieces, Petronela tried to move the fairy display into her room, but Aunt Marzena called her selfish and insisted the display stay where everyone could enjoy it.

Meanwhile, Filomena had helped Petronela discover many of Jolanta's hiding places, and they were stealthily taking all the pieces back.

"Perhaps Papa will allow us time at home together, and I can move all my things back for safekeeping. I only need a change of dress now and then as Aunt Marzena doesn't take me anywhere with her."

The maid touched her cheek. "We can only hope. Be sure to mention you need me with you. The help here is no fun at all. Stiff upper lips, all of them. I'd welcome a day away."

Petronela chose to wait outside at the road—far away from Hortensia and Jolanta who didn't enjoy the outdoors because of the bugs—and close to the bend so she'd see Papa the moment he returned.

Soon, horse hooves *clip-clopped* on the road.

Aunt Marzena's house was the last at the end of the lane, so when only two horses rounded the bend, Petronela quickly focused in on Papa. She waved so hard her arm was like to fall off. He kicked his charger into a canter and pulled away from his companion.

"Petronela!" he lifted his lance in greeting.

He was off his horse before it stopped, and then he scooped her up. He smelled of sweat and dust, but she didn't care. He was home.

He put her down and straightened tall. "Where is everyone else?"

"Oh." *Wasn't she enough?* "They're getting the house ready. The servants have been working all day. You want to go in and say hello before we go home?"

"Home? We're staying here. Didn't your aunt tell you?" He searched the driveway behind her.

"We don't talk much." That was truthful enough, though a twinge of bitterness might have crept into her tone.

Papa turned his attention back to her. "You aren't terribly upset with me about the way I left, are you?"

One day. He was home for one day.

"Yes, but it was clever of you to leave me the fairy village to keep me busy while you were gone."

"I knew you'd love it. Did you share with your cousins?"

Petronela nodded, not trusting her voice to speak. She didn't want to ruin the moment by having to explain Jolanta's theft or Hortensia's rough play that had led to several broken wings and a caved-in roof.

"Excellent. I was hoping the fairies would help you get to know one another better."

"We know one another just fine." She squeezed her thumb to remind herself not to spoil the moment.

"Has the time brought you closer together is what I want to know. Like sisters?"

Petronela couldn't help but make a face. "I'm an only child and perfectly happy with that. Don't worry about me."

Papa pulled the horse's reins and started walking toward the house. "You need more family in your life, Petronela. It's not good for a girl to be raised by a warrior."

"You're only a warrior on the battlefield. At home, you're Papa."

He was turning melancholy again. This happened sometimes when he came home from battle. She knew she shouldn't complain. There'd be plenty of time for truth-telling once Papa was home for good. She'd tell him in a funny way so even when she was complaining, he'd see that she'd made the best of it. Her time with her cousins was her own personal battle.

"Aunt Marzena was happy to have you these past few months. She said it was nice to have a full house."

"She did?" Aunt Marzena spent most of her days in the parlor entertaining her friends. Is that what she meant by a full house?

"In some ways, she is like your mother."

Petronela's throat went dry. *He lies; he knows she is nothing like my mother but he is desperate to fill a hole for me that doesn't need to be filled.* How could she tell him that, yet still keep the conversation positive and happy?

She was aware she was starting to see her father in a new light. Did this mean after these few months apart she was maturing? If so, she didn't like it one bit.

He had convinced himself he was doing what was best for her, yet he had to know how intolerable this family was. He knew how mother felt about her sister, that they were at odds practically from birth. Should Petronela keep pretending that everything was fine in case he did die in the war, which was what he was afraid of?

Or could she convince him she'd be fine no matter what? That the servants could go on maintaining the house, and she could go to school, and it would all be the same, except he wouldn't be there to tell her she was doing a good job.

"Oh, don't get worked up," he said, noticing the tears forming in her eyes.

She blinked rapidly. *My name means rock. I am a rock.*

"You do like your aunt and cousins, don't you?"

Wanting to ease her father's burden, she lied, too. "They are wonderful, Papa." She swallowed the lump in her throat.

He grinned. "I'm so happy to hear that. Marzena and I will be married this afternoon."

CHAPTER 7

*P*etronela stared at the pretty white dress lying on her bed. White as snow and embroidered with highland corn poppies in cheery reds and pinks. The flowered wreath for her hair laid beside it, the cloying scent of carnations turning her stomach.

Marry? What was her father thinking? That meant she would never be free of her cousins. Her visit had been bearable only because she knew it would end.

There was a knock on the door. "Petronela? May I come in to help?"

Petronela flew to the door and then into Filomena's arms.

"There, there. It'll all work out in the end," the servant murmured.

"Why is he getting married? We are fine on our own."

"You know why." Filomena stepped back and then pulled Petronela over to the dress.

"Because he loves her?" Even speaking the words didn't seem right. He loved her mother. How could there be anyone else? Petronela's mother's presence permeated the old house. From her selection of curtains, to her hand-stitched pillowcases. Memories of her were everywhere. If Petronela could get Papa to go home he would see that and come to his senses.

"He may love her, I don't know. I think it's more of an arrangement."

"Because of me."

"Because this war is not over. The men are being moved closer to the heart of the fighting."

Filomena didn't need to explain more. Petronela had thought of it often, and just as often locked the thoughts away in a small corner of her mind. Papa always came home. He would come home again. But the next time he came home, it wouldn't be the two of them. He was changing their future without asking her if she wanted it changed.

"Come now. What will be will be." Filomena held out the dress Petronela was supposed to wear. It matched her cousins' dresses. They'd all look in agreement on the outside even while they were out of step on the inside.

THE WEDDING WAS to take place in the garden, on the patio extending out from the south side of the house.

Where Aunt Marzena had found all those flower arrangements and these matching dresses in such a short time, Petronela would never know. It was as if she'd been planning this day for a very long time.

All through the wedding Petronela marched as if she were a wooden soldier, standing where she was told, sitting with the cousins. Every time her maid caught her attention she would point to her smile, reminding Petronela she was supposed to look happy.

Her cousins looked happy. Petronela supposed they'd had plenty of practice faking their facial expressions.

She heard the guests whispering:

"The child looks sullen. She's being selfish not wanting her father to find happiness again."

"Poor thing, must be tired with all this excitement."

"Dare say Marzena is getting the better end of this bargain. Look at the expense he's gone to. He must have more wealth than we thought."

—"Or he's gone and blown it all to make her happy."

Vows were said. Rings exchanged. Congratulations offered.

The music began, signaling it was time to dance. Petronela released a deep breath. This was her cue that she could go back to her room. It was all over. Her father was married to someone who was not her mother and all she wanted to do was escape and go cry into her pillow.

Instead, Papa came over and held out his hand. "Dance with me."

She looked away. "I don't know how."

"I'll teach you."

Papa's outstretched hand came into her field of vision. She tried to maintain her scowl to show how unhappy she was, but this was Papa. His only night with them, and he wanted to dance with her. She put her hand in his and choked back the tears.

The dancers lined up along the uneven patio bricks, waiting for the bride and groom to begin the dancing. As Petronela walked past them, she tried to ignore the continued whispers.

"It's the first dance; he should be dancing with his wife," said one.

"The bride doesn't look happy; so much for the wedding night," said another.

But Petronela let the wedding guests in the garden fade away, and she danced with her papa. He gave her this dance because he had already given his permission for her to leave when the dancing started and if he waited for the next dance, she'd be gone.

When the waltz was nearly over, Petronela asked, "Will we move back to our house?"

"Er, no. The general has moved in for the duration. It's the only place large enough for him and all the meetings and guests he brings with him."

"Can't they do that at the castle?" All those strangers traipsing around their house while they were gone. Mama's room!

"The king likes to keep the castle removed from things of the war. It's fine. We don't need such a big place anyway. This home works for our needs. Once the war is over, we can return home."

Petronela suffered quietly under this latest blow. She missed her home and all the memories scratched into the wooden floors, embedded into the fabric of the chairs, and frozen into the portraits lining the walls. If the winged warriors all moved in, would it ever feel like her home again?

The song ended and Petronela curtsied while her father bowed. The guests politely clapped, with their attention on Marzena, standing on the edge of the patio. She swooped in, her hand raised for Papa to take it. Petronela turned away and slowly, deliberately walked out of the garden. She felt her maid's gaze follow her, but Petronela refused to look to her for comfort.

CHAPTER 8

*M*onths later, Petronela walked alone into town. She'd made the long trip daily, hoping for news of the war, but there was never anything other than: *It's still going on. No news from your papa.*

Her shoes were wearing thin, so when she passed the cobbler she went in and found a new pair. Simple, sturdy, and with thick soles. So different from the pretty slippers papa last bought her.

"Please credit my papa's account," she told the shopkeeper.

"Sorry, miss. Your father's accounts are due. I can't put anything more on credit. Perhaps you could speak to your mother about settling with me."

"My stepmother."

"Yes, her's the one. Can't put nothing else on credit for her either."

"Of course. I'm sorry." She handed the shoes over and bit her lip as she fled the shop. As she left, she heard the shopkeeper call out.

"Nothing to be sorry about. It's the war. Affects us all."

Accounts were due. *I wonder if Aunt Marzena knows.*

Petronela hovered near the post office and loitered near the mercantile, not going in to buy a small peppermint like she usually did. After her usual inquiries turned up nothing, she determined to press on farther than she had dared before.

There was one location where she might get answers. Papa would know what to do with his accounts. He'd never had problems with them before. If only she could contact him.

She marched through the rest of the town and then down the road to her house, where she hadn't dared to venture since she left it months ago.

A young soldier stood at the gate picking a weed apart and throwing the pieces into the wind. When he saw Petronela approach, he stood at attention.

"Aron!" She ran toward him. "When did you enter the service?"

Her heart saddened as she studied his crisp uniform. He was too young to be a soldier. Had they really lost so many young men to the war?

He scowled. "I'm not officially a soldier. They made me come up to the road when I complained about how they were treating the animals."

She gasped. "They've mistreated the animals?"

"Don't worry. I sent the cows to the Kowalskis, the horses your aunt didn't take are with the Mazurs over in the next valley. Only the chickens stay because they want the daily eggs, and those chickens can hold their own." He lifted his hat and scratched his head. "I sent you word."

"Oh. I haven't gotten any messages. Thank you for taking care of the animals. I knew we could trust you with them."

He nodded, looking too old and wise for his age in that proper shirt. "How've you been? Heard your papa got married."

"Yes. You've met my aunt."

He nodded. "Sure have."

"Then you know how I've been."

"Anything I can do for you?"

"You can let me pass."

Aron whistled low. "Can't do that. My job is to let people through who are on the list, and them only." He pointed to a clipboard at his feet.

"It's my house."

He had the decency to look away. "Yes, well. Still can't."

"What do you do when it rains?" she asked.

"What?" He wrinkled his brow as he looked at the sky.

"You need a shelter. Your clipboard's going to get wet."

He laughed. "Ever the practical one. Yes, a shelter would be nice. They give me wide-brimmed hat on rainy days."

"When I talk to whomever's in charge I'll put in a word about building a gatehouse for you."

He deflated. "Nela, I can't."

She put her hands on her hips. "You know I can get around you. May as well let me pass and save me the time of outrunning you." She doubted they had added a fence all the way around the property, and even if they did, she knew where the stream cut across and how she could get in that way.

"Fine. But when you get close to the house, don't march down the middle of the road like you own the place. Come in from the woods so it looks like I turned you away and you snuck in."

"Of course." She waved as she walked onto her own property.

Petronela made it to the kitchen without anyone stopping her. Very few vehicles were parked out front, so it may be that those in charge had moved closer to the fighting, and this trip would be wasted. Except, it was so good to be home, even if she felt like an intruder as she cracked open the back door.

Immediately she noticed the kitchen had been rearranged. An oversize plank table in the center dominated the space and made it look like a mess hall. Filomena would be pleased to know the floor was swept and clean dishes stacked in rows. The army was nothing if not neat.

Before anyone could walk in and discover her, she darted into the pantry. From here, she could access the secret servants' doors the general likely didn't know about. She'd be able to walk within the walls unnoticed.

The usual shelves of peach preserves and jars of sauerkraut were replaced with military rations and canned beans. She tugged on the shelf that was the secret door, and it squeaked in protest as it opened. She quickly slipped inside and closed it behind her. If the noise brought someone to investigate, hopefully they would assume it was a mouse trying to steal a bite to eat.

Petronela remained frozen in the dark, waiting. When no one entered the pantry, she felt around for the maids' supply of candles. There was one. And the matches. The wick flamed to life, illuminating the gray-brick passageway.

Filomena had let her play in the narrow spaces, and so Petronela knew where each of the passageways went. She assumed the general would set up in her father's office, and quietly made her way there.

Deep voices muffled through the walls indicated she was correct. She pressed her ear against the cold wall. There were at least two different voices, but she couldn't make out the words they were saying. If she were to hear anything at all, she'd have to get closer somehow. The passageways weren't meant for spying, but for silent service.

First, she'd sneak upstairs and visit her room.

Even though this was her home, her heart raced like she imagined a thief's would when sneaking around. With the flickering candle giving her just enough light to keep her from tripping up the stairs, she quietly made her way to the second floor. She held the candle close to the wall until it illuminated the crack revealing the door that opened into her bedroom. She pressed her ear against the rough-cut side of the door and listened. It sounded empty, so she gently pushed the door open. When there was no startled response, she opened the door fully and stepped inside the room.

Enough bunk beds lined the walls to accommodate eight soldiers. Bunk beds in her room.

She'd never had bunk beds, though she'd always wondered what it would be like to have siblings. *I suppose I have siblings now.* They weren't nearly as fun as she'd imagined they would be.

The only items of hers that remained were the lace curtains that hopefully reminded the men that they were squatters here. Surely, they put her belongings in storage. What a strange thought: a group of military men packing up all the little-girl things she'd kept all these years. The rocking horse, the dolls. Mementos of her life with Mama.

Mama's room!

Petronela exited her room through the hallway, cautiously listening for where everyone was in the house before tiptoeing down the hall. She tried the door, but it was locked. Maybe Papa had told them they could have the whole house as long as they left this room alone. After mama's death, he'd even moved to the smaller bedroom at the end of the hall so the room would be preserved the way Mama had left it.

Still, Petronela had to know for sure.

She slipped back into the walls and entered her mother's room through the closet. Immediately, she knew something was off. The smell was wrong.

The door wasn't locked to preserve her mother's memory.

She stared at the pile of armor in the middle of the floor and the special Hussar lances stacked alongside. Mother's things had been shoved against the wall.

How dare they? Of all the rooms to desecrate. They had no right. Papa would have told them not to use this room. It was time to talk to whomever was in charge.

She thumped angrily down the staircase, announcing her presence.

Within seconds, three military men had raced out of her father's office and met her at the bottom of the stairs.

"How did you get in here?" the tallest one asked.

"Who are you?" asked the one in the middle.

None of them had their jackets on so she couldn't tell if any of them were the general.

"This is my house." She lifted her chin. "I was looking for information on my father's whereabouts."

"Dominik's daughter?" They looked uneasily at one another.

The first man who spoke winced slightly. "We sent a dispatch to your house this morning. Didn't you receive it?"

"No. I was in town." Her voice faltered. "What is it? Is he all right?"

The one who had yet to speak cleared his throat. "Your father was injured in battle and was in medical transport back here when he passed away. I'm sorry."

Petronela cocked her head as she silently repeated the words, trying to make sense of them. Her thoughts moved so slowly, like they were stuck in honey.

"Can I get you something? Some water?" The first man asked.

She shook her head, even though her mouth had gone dry. "No. I'll just go up to my room." She turned and started walking back upstairs.

The middle man jumped up after her, blocking the stairs. "I'm sorry, miss, but you can't do that. It's not your room at the moment."

"What?" She blinked at him, then remembered. The men's clothes. The shaving instruments on her dresser. The bunk beds. "Right. Of course." She spoke mechanically and turned around.

She looked up at the stained-glass oak tree above the front door. "Mother made that window. She was incredibly artistic. In the end, she was too weak to finish soldering the final pieces on her tree, so Papa finished it for her. Then he carried her in and set her down on the stairs beside me so we could watch him install it. That's my final memory of her. She died later that night." With this memory, the fog surrounding her thoughts started to clear and a wave of emotion began to build.

The men all exchanged uncomfortable looks. The one blocking her stood out of her way and cleared his throat. "May I see you home?"

Back to her stepmother and cousins. By now, they would know, too.

"No. I need the time alone, please." She didn't want to break down in front of these men. She needed to flee. To run to her special place in the woods.

As she burst out the kitchen door, she heard one of the men say, "No. Let her go."

Past the stables and down to the ravine, she ran until her lungs burned. Here, the shrubbery and forest detritus remained undisturbed by the army. She stopped for a breath at a smooth rock where she sat.

Papa had planned for this. He had made sure Petronela was settled. *Oh, Papa. You've left me utterly alone.*

Through her tears she saw tiny sticks poking up in a circle to create the foundation of a gazebo, the roof missing. Remnants of the little fairy garden she'd built the last time she was here.

If only she lived in a world where fairies were real.

CHAPTER 9

The walk to her aunt's house was slow and long, and though Petronela was somewhat aware that her legs were tired after covering such distance in one day, she wished she could have walked longer. She wasn't finished processing all she'd learned that day, but she had nowhere to go.

She was an orphan.

Everyone who loved her in this world was gone.

If she could slip unspotted into her room, she would be able to grieve on her own. The way it should be. Thankfully, no one met her at the door of her aunt's house. She stealthily made her way up to her room, but when she got there, had no reason to rejoice. Her stepmother and cousins were already there, a pile of clothes lying in the middle of the floor, and her stepmother at the closet pulling out more.

"What are you doing?" Petronela balled her hands into fists as she burst into the room.

Aunt Marzena spun on her, face flush not with tears, but anger. "You have no say here."

"But—"

"There is no money. What he hasn't spent on you he gave to the king to fight this war." Aunt Marzena shoved the closet door open wider and yanked out more clothes for the pile on the floor. Her daughters hovered near the bed, mouths agape. "All this frivolity wasted on a child. And these clothes are so small you can't even share them with my girls. A disgrace."

Petronela ran forward and tried to save her things. "These are mine. You'll ruin them."

Aunt Marzena tore a silk gown out of Petronela's hand, ripping the lace off the bodice. She threw it into the pile. "Ungrateful child. How am I to support you, now? These must be sold so we can eat."

Jolanta blanched. "Is it really that serious, Mama?"

"The three of us know how to live simply. Petronela will have to learn as well."

Petronela glanced at Hortensia's new lace-trimmed dress while breathing in Jolanta's sickly sweet perfume from Paris. When had they ever lived simply?

"Of course, I'll do what I can to help." Petronela bowed her head slightly to appease Marzena. Meanwhile, her thoughts whirled. Father wanted her here. Wanted her to be protected upon his death. She would watch and wait.

"Good. Because I've already dismissed your servant and sold that childish fairy set. You were much too old for that anyway. I don't know what your father was thinking when he gave it to you."

Petronela sucked in a breath. That was her last gift from him. She ran to the playroom. The table where the little houses and happy fairies had lived was wiped clean. It was as if Jolanta had stolen everything all at once instead of bit by bit.

"They came for it while you were gone." Hortensia sidled up to her, her face smug.

Petronela lifted her chin, keeping her eyes clear and her

mouth firm. She would not react. She would not let Hortensia know how much she bled inside.

"Is Filomena still here? I'd like to say goodbye."

"She tried to hang around—said she wanted to wait for you—but we think she was waiting for us to turn our backs, so she could take the silverware with her." Hortensia crossed her arms.

"They've all left except for the cook." Jolanta slumped against the wall, looking despondent.

Petronela clenched her hands while she calmly turned and walked down the stairs, out the front door, and into the stables. No one would follow her here since they didn't like the smell.

They didn't like anything except for themselves.

Instead of offering her comfort—at the very least the polite way to act—they had taken turns trying to make her feel worse. *Oh, Papa. What am I to do on my own?* She whispered it aloud and the chestnut horse flicked his tail. She found a brush and began to groom him. It was good to have a task to focus on, even if it was unnecessary.

She chatted with the horses and sat in the hay until she thought the rest of the household would be finished with her room and busy preparing for supper by changing into their evening dresses.

She crept into the quiet house and back up to her bedroom where she gently closed the door before flinging herself onto the bed. She wouldn't bother showing up for the meal. She'd sneak some food out of the kitchen when she got hungry.

Her privacy was short-lived as Jolanta followed her in.

"Thought that was you I heard. It's usually Hortensia sneaking past my room. I've gotten good about hearing that one squeaky board. Helps me to have something to hold over her."

Petronela ignored her until Jolanta cleared her throat, making Petronela glance up.

Her cousin pulled the blue-clad fairy out of her pocket and held it out. "Good thing I took it before they came. I know it was your favorite." She had the courtesy to blush. "That's why I nicked it."

"Thank you." What a surprise to feel grateful for Jolanta's stealing. Petronela reached for it but Jolanta pulled it away. "I just wanted you to know I have it. Maybe you could earn it back from me by doing some of the work the servants did, that sort of thing." She smiled sweetly. "You better get moving. Mama sent me to tell you you're needed in the kitchen. It's time to serve supper."

CHAPTER 10

*N*adzia waved one last time to Esmerelda, who stood in the doorway at the cottage.

"I'll be fine," she said, even though she was too far away to be heard. She spun forward to face her future and her confidence rose with the early-morning sun over the mountains. She was going to market—alone!—with her bag filled with tatted lace to sell. She thought back to all those years ago, to her very first trip to town for her ribbons. The sights and smells had made such a deep impression on her. She and Esmerelda had gone many times since then, but now was another first. Going alone.

In the quiet moments at the cottage, she and Esmerelda made fantastical lace using only simple thread and a tatting shuttle. Of course, Esmerelda's lace was so much better than hers, as Nadzia was only learning.

Early on she wrestled with the thread while trying to flip the knot correctly, but once she'd caught on, she loved it. There was something satisfying in seeing the numbers and lines Esmerelda wrote down for her be tatted into dainty lace. Esmerelda didn't need a pattern, but she'd written several for Nadzia, who kept forgetting the order. Numbers seemed to fly out of her head the moment they entered.

Once Nadzia was out of sight of the cabin, she glanced back for movement. It would be so like Esmerelda to secretly follow to make sure she didn't get lost. Sensing nothing, she grinned to the birds. "Lovely morning, isn't it?" She tipped her head at a robin. How could she get lost when there was only one main path? Stick to the path and she'd end up in town. Easy.

A small portion of the money she made today would go towards buying oscypki cheese to trade with the over-mountain peddler. He'd be at the cottage this week for his last visit before the risk of snowfall that would make the mountains impassable.

Oscypki was his favorite, but she and Esmerelda hadn't made any since his last visit. The wooden molds that turned goats' milk into loaves resembling bread had remained unused on top of the cabinet because Esmerelda wanted them to focus their energies on the lace. Many of the villagers made their own cheese, but not as many made lace.

She ran part of the way, eager to get to town. But when beads of sweat began to form along her hairline, she slowed to a walk, concerned about making the right impression. Would the other craftswomen smile and make room for her at one of the shared tables? Esmerelda said they would, especially if she gave them each a sample bookmark as a thank you for helping her on her first day.

As Nadzia neared the town, she quickened her gait again. The sun was too high in the sky. She feared the market had already started, and once sellers had spread out on the tables, it would be difficult to convince them to make room for her.

The castle came into view again. Up on the mountain, it towered over the town. Made of strong granite blocks and decorated with bright red flags bearing the white eagle, it was a constant reminder of the king quietly watching over them.

The royal family was known for being reclusive. Some said it was the death of the heir, the eldest prince, that drove them into even deeper seclusion. That once, craftsmen were allowed to visit the castle to show their wares, and villagers with disagreements could meet in the council room for judgment. But now all common business took place in town. According to Esmerelda, the king, queen, and surviving prince were rarely seen.

Nadzia looked in dismay at the milling crowd. As she'd suspected, the marketplace was already humming. Quickly, she assessed the stalls and open tables. The covered stalls were understood to belong to the townsfolk who were regulars to market, but who didn't have their own shops. The open tables were used by folk like her, who saved up wares to come to market once in a while. And they were already filled with jams and mushrooms and cheese.

Nadzia walked the length, holding up her bag so they knew she was a vendor, and waited for someone to meet her with a smile. Finally, at the end, a large woman with a friendly gaze waved her over.

"New here?"

"Yes. I've got lace to sell."

"Oo. Let's see it, hun." She reached over and pawed through the bag. "Lovely. Why don't you set up by me?" With a sweep of her arm she'd squeezed her honey jars together, giving Nadzia half the space.

"Thank you." Remembering Esmerelda's advice, she handed the woman her prettiest bookmark. "For your kindness."

"Lovely, just lovely. You should do well today if any of the *ladies* come to market."

Soon, Nadzia understood what the honey seller meant by ladies. The first few hours she sold only one small piece of lace to a woman who was working across the square. That woman sold hats and planned to add the lace to one of them. Most folks came to market to buy necessities, not finery. Perhaps Esmerelda was wrong in choosing lace over cheese.

But in the afternoon, a different sort of buyer arrived. These were the fancy ladies. Those who already had the necessities and were looking for finer things. Nadzia's tatting was a novelty and soon a crowd gathered around. The honey seller, having sold out her supply earlier in the day, switched to helping Nadzia keep track of who had paid and who hadn't.

"This is all you have?" asked one woman, who had arrived late. She cast Nadzia an annoyed look.

"It is one of the prettier pieces," said the honey seller, stepping in. "I had set it aside for myself whilst I decided if I wanted it or not." She held out her hand like she expected the woman to give it to her.

The woman clutched the lace to her chest. "I'll take it."

As the happy customer walked away, Nadzia grinned at the honey seller, her new friend. "Thank you for your help today."

"Any time you want to share my table, I'll make room. Now, I best get back to the family. Make sure the young'uns haven't destroyed the place."

"And I need to buy some cheese before it's all gone." They parted ways and Nadzia hurried over to the cheese seller she'd seen doing the most business.

In her haste she bumped another shopper into a pile of cabbages, which spilled onto the ground around the shopper's bare feet.

"I'm sorry. I didn't see you," Nadzia said. Thoroughly embarrassed, she rushed to pick up the cabbages.

"It's fine," said the young woman, though the cabbage seller frowned at the two of them while they cleaned up the mess.

When the girl handed the last one to Nadzia, a memory was tickled.

The girl looked so familiar. *Who was she?* She had blond hair pulled back into braids and then twisted in a bun at the nape of her neck. She wore a brown dress that had seen much wear, covered by a freshly washed, but stained apron.

Nadzia knew so few people, it was an odd sensation to recognize a stranger. She walked away, glancing back to see the girl continue to haggle with a seller over the price of herbs.

The feeling to help the girl was so strong, she hung back until the girl walked away without any herbs.

"I know where you can get a better price," she said.

The girl stopped to talk. "Where? The growing season is ending."

"We grow herbs up in the mountains in a small glass house. I didn't know we could sell them at market here. Esmerelda gives them away to those who make it as far as our place. Except, it's rather far. And I should probably ask before I invite you. Esmerelda likes to be alone." *But I don't. It would be so nice to have a girl closer to my age to talk to.* She smiled with as big a welcoming smile as she could make.

"It was kind of you to offer. Maybe next time you're in town?"

"I don't come often."

"Right, because it's far."

"Follow the eastern path up into the mountains until you think you can't go any farther. Then keep going and you'll find us. A little cottage near a small stream." As an afterthought, she added. "We have a goat."

The girl smiled now, for the first time in their conversation.

"A goat. Thank you."

CHAPTER 11

"Are you sure it was the girl in the carriage?" Esmerelda sorted beans while listening to the details of the previous day. She was pleased with Nadzia's first trip alone, and even more pleased that Nadzia might have found a way to make a living. Once she was taken care of, Esmerelda could move along, like she'd been itching to do for years.

"Positive. When she handed me the cabbage, it was like when she gave me the ribbon, but I didn't remember until I was on my way home. We were meant to meet again. I think she needs help. She didn't look good at all. Well, I mean, she looked fine, except for her raggedy clothes, and she was too thin for a girl her age."

"She's had a reversal of fortune."

Esmerelda felt a stirring in her bones stronger than the itching in her feet. It'd been a while since she'd helped out a girl. *The fairy godmother way.*

Nadzia leaned against the table. "I suppose she has. Going from riding in that fancy carriage to walking barefoot through the market. But she's as kind as she was the first time we met."

"Poor dear. Hope she keeps her wits about her."

"She seems to be. May I go back to town and bring her some

of our herbs? Herbs seemed very important for some reason."

"I'll go. Find out what's going on."

"You?" Nadzia frowned. "I was hoping…"

"I know what you were hoping. And next time you can be the one to go. The animals will need tending while I'm gone. Did she tell you where she was living now?"

"No, but she kept looking west of town. Think it might be out that way?"

"I'll start there. Help me pack." Esmerelda took down the large woven basket hanging from the ceiling and began filling it with a variety of herbs.

"That's not too heavy for you?" Nadzia called out from the doorway.

Esmerelda smiled. It was very heavy. "No, dearie, I'm fine. Go in now. No use watching me waddle down the lane."

Nadzia waved, then slowly shut the door.

"Your time is coming," Esmerelda whispered to Nadzia as she walked away from the cottage. *I've gotten used to the girl, but she's almost grown. It'll be time for her to find other arrangements soon.*

She lugged the basket until she was beyond the first rise, then let it drop. "Well, that's enough of that." She pulled out her wand and waved it around herself and the basket. In a swirl of glitter, she was transported to the outskirts on the western side of town. "That's better."

She picked up the basket and walked on to the first house. She entered through the gate, climbed the porch, but noticing the well-tended garden, knew she wasn't in the right place. As she turned, the woman of the house rounded the corner. She took one look at Esmerelda's mountain costume and made shooing motions with her hands.

"Don't need anything you're selling."

"Know anyone who does?" Esmerelda kept her composure, though she was sorely tempted to turn the woman into a croaky toad.

"Woman up the lane has a sickly child. Always trying various teas to make her feel better."

"Thank you."

Maybe that was it, the child looked poorly because she was ill. But why would her mother send her out to do the shopping?

Once she was out of sight of the neighbor, Esmerelda waved her wand again and landed outside the door of a stately house at the end of a long meandering dirt road. *This one can't be right, either. It's too fancy.* She glanced up at the lovely stained-glass window above the door. An expansive oak tree set against a blue sky.

She looked all around, and clues made themselves known. The yard was overgrown, though the bushes looked like someone had attempted to rein them in. Barns in the back leaned in the direction of the wind, and the gingerbread trim on the house looked like it needed a fresh coat of paint. There was a story to tell here, for sure. Just what kind would it be?

Esmerelda hefted the basket up the stairs to the front door. She used the round knocker to bang nice and loud. She did like to make an entrance.

After a moment's wait, a middle-aged woman appeared. She examined Esmerelda up and down before saying in clipped tones, "What do you want?"

"To help you, ma'am. I've both fresh and dried herbs, along with the knowledge of how to use them."

"Where did you come from? You aren't carrying any diseases from the mountains, are you?"

Esmerelda glanced at her thick, homespun tunic. If these folks only knew how warm and practical the mountain clothing was, they wouldn't complain so much.

"You can use my wares in your cooking, in teas, or in healing remedies."

"There's a bug crawling in there." The woman curled her lip

while swatting her hand back and forth near the basket. "Take your filthy wares elsewhere. We buy from the market."

Esmerelda fought to not roll her eyes.

"What do you have there, miss?" A thin, pale girl walked behind the lady in the foyer while balancing a laundry basket on her hip. "I wasn't able to buy comfrey at market today."

There she was. Nadzia's little princess, now looking like a servant girl. She appeared well enough. No longer the bright, rosy child, but a young woman and likely another victim of the consequences of war.

Annoyed, the woman of the house turned inside, blocking Esmerelda's view. "If we buy from her," she whispered, "she'll only come back. We don't need the likes of her coming around. And is that how loudly you ask for it in the market? Telling everyone our secrets?"

"I've comfrey somewhere in here." Esmerelda made a show of looking through her basket. She plunked it on the ground and began removing great clumps of herbs and spreading them out across the doorway.

"Oh, for goodness sakes, not here. We're expecting company. See what you did?" The woman took a swat at the girl, who was too quick for her, dashing upstairs with her basket, and then she was gone.

"I've also got yarrow for your problem." Esmerelda lifted her eyebrows knowingly.

The woman's own eyes grew wide and a faint blushed appeared.

"Get. Off with you. And don't come here again." The woman closed the door with a note of finality in the click of its lock.

Hmph. Now how was she going to gather more information about the girl? Esmerelda slowly lumped all her herbs into the basket and took her time going down the stairs.

She had already shuffled halfway down the lane when the girl chased after her.

"Excuse me! Wait!" the girl called.

Esmerelda smiled and turned around. She dropped the basket at her feet and waited.

"Is someone sick in your home?" she asked the girl.

"Not life or death, as you'd think. Hortensia has acne, and all the soldiers are coming home for good, now that there's finally a peace agreement after all these years. Her mother plans to marry her off."

Esmerelda smothered a smile. "I see." *Common vanity.* "And what about you?"

"Me? What about me?"

"The soldiers are returning. Aren't you interested in that?"

The girl shrugged. "I haven't thought about it. I'm too tired from chores to make time for dancing and romance. Someone has to do the work around here."

"You do it all?"

"Most of it." She looked around, her eyes focusing on the disused barns. "As much as I can. It was my father's home, and I know he'd want me to keep it up."

"That woman isn't your mother?"

"No. That's some consolation." The girl pointed to the basket. "What is your price? I'm fine with any damaged pieces, prefer those, in fact. Hortensia will not be happy when she finds out I couldn't buy any in the marketplace."

Esmerelda gave her price and the girl eagerly took it.

"And why do you want to help this Hortensia?"

"It means one less bothersome girl in the house if we can help her find love. That's worth all the comfrey in the world to me." She smiled a mischievous grin. "Not sure what herb it'll take to move Jolanta along, but I'm working on that."

They shared a smile before the girl spun around to return home.

Esmerelda watched for a moment, wondering when and how she would be called upon to help this plucky girl.

CHAPTER 12

*P*etronela smelled her new bundle of herbs as she watched the mountain woman amble down the lane. She should have asked the herb seller if she knew the young girl she'd met in the village—the friendly one who talked about the herbs she grew up the mountain. It seemed like they were of the same temperament and might know each other. Perhaps she would meet one or both of them again if she found herself in need of more herbs.

She quickly returned to the kitchen via the back of the house before Marzena could guess what she'd done. No sooner had she stored the comfrey in a crock when the doorbell rang, signaling the tutor was there.

Aunt Marzena had sold the piano to pay for etiquette lessons for the girls. She sold the paintings for new clothes, and the crystal for new hair. If Aunt Marzena had her way, her daughters would be completely remade girls by the end of the week.

Petronela scurried to the door, knowing how irritated her aunt must've been about having to open it earlier for the herb seller.

"Petronela! Get that!" Marzena called.

Petronela let out a breath before she opened the door. *I was right here*, she wanted to yell back. A cool wind swirled into the entry room along with the tutor. He dressed in green wool pants of the style from across the mountains. Petronela took a step back, surprised at his blatancy for wearing those colors on *this* side of the mountain.

He fidgeted, tugging at his neckline until he settled on the fact that Petronela was a serving girl. Then he lost the fake smile under his thick mustache and asked for the lady of the house.

"Wait in here." She led him into the sitting room where she left him to critique the furnishings while she went to find her aunt.

Irritatingly, Marzena had hidden herself in the study, knowing full well she'd be wanted at the door.

"He's from over the mountain." Petronela crossed her arms accusingly. Her father had died in the war against the people over the mountain, and now her aunt was welcoming a tutor, bold enough to wear the colors of their rivals, to come and teach her daughters. *Teach them what, exactly?*

"Where did you put him?"

"In the sitting room, where we greet all our guests."

Petronela knew Aunt Marzena wanted her to act like a proper servant, but Petronela just couldn't. She'd cook and clean as needed for the upkeep of the house, but she would not cower and obey every ridiculous and demeaning command she was given. She wasn't a servant, she was family and this was *her* home no matter how possessive the others acted.

"Excellent. My daughters must be prepared for positions of influence and everyone says this man is the best tutor on either side of the mountain. Go get the girls, and then tend to the flues. We'll need to start the fires soon."

"Yes, ma'am."

Petronela wanted to follow Marzena to the sitting room to

listen to their exchange, but her aunt sat at her desk waiting for Petronela to leave the room first.

Petronela dropped her arms to her sides and went to find the girls. Hortensia smiled and ran off quickly, but Jolanta made a face like she was eating squash, her least favorite food. "Do I have to go?" she asked.

"She's your mother. Do whatever you like."

Jolanta rolled her eyes. "I never get to do what I like. They want to refine me so I'll catch a man's eye. I'd rather stay here with you. You make such fine breakfasts." She smiled like an idea had just occurred to her. "If I marry, will you be my cook?"

Petronela about choked. Did Jolanta actually think she was a servant to be passed around from household to household? "You better go," she said. "They're waiting for you."

"Right. But don't let Hortensia steal you away." She spun out of the room in a whoosh of skirts. "I asked first."

Once she was alone, Petronela let out a deep sigh. The sooner she could rid herself of those two, the better. Now, to tackle the fireplaces.

She gathered her supplies from the maid's closet and lugged them to Papa's old room. May as well start in the room that would matter most to her aunt. Tall and angular, Marzena had no fat on her bones to help her stay warm. She wore a shawl, even in the summer, so a working fireplace was important to her.

Thankfully, when they'd come to the house after the military had vacated it, even Marzena was not so bold as to move into Mama's old room, though it still irked to have her living in Papa's room.

Petronela spread an old sheet at the base of the fireplace. After lighting a candle, she opened the flue and shone the light up into the darkness. The flame was instantly swallowed up. Not that she was an expert at chimney cleaning, but she hoped all it would take was a quick poke with the brush.

She shoved the thick bristles up the chimney, hoping this was all she would need to do. No way was she going up on the roof. Aunt Marzena would just have to hire someone. Sell her fancy four poster bed if she needed to.

"Petronela!"

Startled, Petronela jerked the brush down instead of being slow and careful. A cloud of ash and soot tumbled out and all over her and the sheet. In dismay, she watched as the black cloud billowed around the room. Aunt Marzena would be furious. And Petronela would have to wash all the bedding again.

She shook as much off herself as she could, but the cries of "Petronela!" shrieked louder.

"Yes, what?" she asked, coming to a stop in the sitting room. Hortensia and Jolanta stood awkwardly in front of the window, in the middle of reciting a poem they had been working on. The tutor's pinched face showed he was not amused.

Aunt Marzena turned to give orders, but instead made a squeaking noise. The girls burst out laughing, and the tutor merely blinked, bewildered.

"What happened to you?" Aunt Marzena finally said.

Hortensia continued giggling. "It looks like you've fallen into the cinders."

"Cindernela!" Jolanta laughed at her joke.

Petronela glanced down at her clothes which she'd shaken reasonably clean, but then touched her face. Her fingers came away coated with soot. Had something like this occurred back when father was alive and Aron caught her in a mess of chimney soot, she'd have thought it was funny, too. But not the way they were all sneering at her.

"You called, Aunt Marzena?"

"I was going to ask you to put out afternoon tea, but given your current condition," Marzena looked disapprovingly down her nose, "never mind. Go back to the chimneys. Jolanta can serve us."

"Me?" Jolanta immediately stopped laughing. "But I'm hungry

now, and I don't know how to serve."

Aunt Marzena held her hand to her forehead. "I may have been hasty sending that mountain woman away. In the morning, Petronela, go and purchase some yarrow for me. Take the sheep with you. They can eat for free up there."

Marzena had sold all the other animals, but for whatever reason kept her handful of sheep. They were more trouble than they were worth since the sheepdog had also been sold. Petronela preferred to keep them penned in their small meadow so she could keep track of them easier.

"How am I to find this mountain woman who sells herbs?"

"Shouldn't be hard. There aren't many living up there anymore."

"But there was frost on the ground this morning. Higher up, there might be snow already. That's not good for your sheep."

"My sheep will be fine. In fact, the cold will make their coats grow even thicker. Perhaps you should make daily trips up there for the next month."

Petronela bit her lip and left the room. She knew to argue meant more needless work piled on her. Although, spending every day up in the mountains and away from her family might not be a bad way to spend the time. Peaceful, and it would give her time to think and to plan.

Hortensia followed her out and furtively tucked some money into Petronela's apron pocket. "And the comfrey?" Although it didn't look as if it were doing any good. Hortensia would be better off if she quit sneaking sugary treats and got outside in the sun once in a while. Not that Hortensia would ever take advice from her.

"Yes. I'll try." She didn't say she'd already bought some that day for the best price she'd ever managed. Whenever she could, Petronela squirreled away what remained of her father's money. Bit by bit her savings added up, a backup plan if ever she had to be the one to leave the house.

CHAPTER 13

"*P*leasure, as always," the peddler said to Esmerelda and Nadzia as he slipped on his thick wool jacket. "But I must be off. These old bones tell me we are in for an early winter this year." He held his hands over Esmerelda's crackling wood stove one last time.

Nadzia's own fingers and toes had been cold from the moment she woke up, so she nodded in agreement. "My young bones say you're right."

"I've lived in these mountains my whole life. I smell the changes on the wind. It was good to see you all again. Shame our kingdoms have been at odds of late."

"The minds of kings," Esmerelda mused, handing him packages to stuff into his large backpack.

He held up one of the small bundles. "Sure you can't share the recipe? What am I going to do when I'm too old to cross the mountain pass and come for my favorite cheese? My brother's sheep would love to have their milk made into oscypki."

Esmerelda shook her head. "Kingdom secret. I won't be the one to share it."

Meanwhile, Nadzia slipped on a pair of gloves and a knit hat.

Tea would be a welcome treat when she returned from walking the peddler to the mountain pass.

"You don't have to come with me," he said, noticing she was beginning to bundle up.

"I want to." Janosik was getting older, and it would be her pleasure to help him cross a particularly steep part of the mountain to make sure he got through without a fall. She would never tell him so, though. "We get few visitors up here, and I like to get as much talking in as I can." And that was the truth.

Janosik tugged on his red knit hat before opening the door. He whistled to his sheepdog who eagerly came running with his tail wagging. "That's a good boy, Bobik. Ready to go home?"

They set out at a relaxed pace.

Nadzia breathed in the fresh air and reflected on the change of season. Her mountain home was lovely, and Esmerelda so dear. But it would be wonderful to go into town more often. Meet more people. Maybe get to know that poor girl and count her as a friend.

Sometimes, at the end of the day, Nadzia could tell Esmerelda wasn't interested in talking anymore, but there were so many things on Nadzia's mind that she needed to let out.

When the snows came, they'd essentially be cut off from everyone until spring. It wasn't that the trail was impassable, but that it was cold and cumbersome. Snowshoes were a must and avalanches a constant threat.

Yesterday, she'd harvested most of what was left in the garden. The last of the cabbage and carrots and turnips. The growing season was over, and it was time to fill up the root cellar and finish the last of the canning. It would be a busy work day once she returned.

Janosik broke their companionable silence. "You're quiet for a girl who said she had lots to talk about."

She smiled. "Maybe I'm picking up Esmerelda's peaceful ways. How long have you known her?"

"Long time. I knew her before you came along. She's never minded my reputation. I've got a bit of a history—until a fortuitous meeting with an injured clergyman near the pass who made me rethink the path I was on. I like to think I ended up deserving of her friendship."

"Did she tell you how I ended up at her place?"

"Yes. Do you know the story?"

She glanced sideways. "You are wise not to tell secrets, but yes, I know about being left in a basket." They'd reached the steep part of the path, and Nadzia looped her arm through the old man's. "One day, I would love to find my mother and learn about any family, but we've looked, and she won't be found." And *Esmerelda doesn't want me to think of herself as my mother, even though in my heart, I do.*

Janosik patted her hand. "Esmerelda had me look on my side of the mountain, too. I have found no one either."

"You did?" Her heart expanded with more love for their kind neighbor. "Thank you for trying. I'm reasonably content to leave that part of my life as a mystery."

"Reasonably?"

She laughed. "We don't always get what we want, do we?" She was teasing him about wanting the cheese recipe, but was also speaking to herself. Esmerelda had tried, and if Esmerelda couldn't find the mother, how could Nadzia herself?

They continued on in silence until they neared the pass between the kingdoms. Even though there was a peace treaty, Esmerelda would not allow her to go any farther than the outcrop of boulders shaped like a tower.

"I'm sorry I was so reflective today," she said. "Not very companionable after all."

"You are at that age," he said. "Reaching for independence. Happens to the best of us."

He stumbled and Nadzia tightened her grip.

The dog whined his concern, and Janosik chuckled ruefully.

"Then we age too much and start to lose our independence. We become like children again." He scratched behind the dog's ear. "Even Bobik watches out for me."

"Nonsense, you're as strong as a mountain goat."

He patted her hand. "If you ever need my help, I'm the first cabin you'll come to. Although for the next few weeks you'll find me in some *bacowka*, the shepherd's hut, gathering supplies for the winter. I'd like to repay the favor if I ever can."

Perhaps she and Esmerelda weren't so sly with their assistance to him, after all.

She waved until he disappeared, and then she ran back to the cottage.

"Janosik well on his way?" Esmerelda carried a full basket of produce on her hip up from the garden.

"Yes. He made it just fine, only one stumble."

"I'm glad you went with him, then. He's been a faithful friend."

"Speaking of friends," Nadzia took the basket from Esmerelda before they reached the cottage. "I keep thinking about that girl from town. Can't we do something for her? She's been so kind to me and seems like she's in a bad place now."

Esmerelda fiddled with the amber necklace at her throat. "What do you suggest? Since the war ended, there are sorry people on both sides of the mountain. Recovery is coming. We all have to be patient."

"I suppose. But I still want to think of something. We could do it secretly and pretend we're her fairy godmothers like in the old stories you've taught me."

"Yes, well." Esmerelda fanned her face. "Why don't you get started on those vegetables." She sat down hard in her chair. "I'll catch my breath for a moment."

Nadzia set the basket beside the sink. It was already afternoon and she was tired from the long walk. She opened the window above the sink so the cool breeze would keep her awake while she processed the harvest.

Baa. The bleat of a sheep came through the open window. *Baa* came another.

Nadzia pushed her head outside the window. Three sheep with the beginnings of their winter coats walked in a row down the path, the girl from the market not far behind.

"It's her! She found us." Nadzia turned and raised her eyebrows. It was what Esmerelda would call *providential.* "Now, can we help her?"

Esmerelda returned the grin. "We can at least feed her. Tea and what else?"

"Wish we had biscuits. I'll go get her." Nadzia flew out the door, hands waving to get the girl's attention.

The little princess turned sheepherder grinned and waved back.

"Hello! Welcome to our mountain," Nadzia called out.

"Happy to be here."

The girl tilted her face to the sun as if all her burdens had slipped away from her. What a sad but hopeful picture. Nadzia wondered if the girl knew how much she revealed in her expressions and demeanor. The scene dug into Nadzia's heart, and she wanted to help more than ever.

"We've put tea on. Would you like a cup?"

"You are too kind," the girl called back.

When they caught up to each other, Nadzia introduced herself and added, "I'm so glad you came."

"I'm Petronela. You don't mind my sheep grazing here?"

"Not at all. They look content in our meadow, so you can visit while they eat."

"I'd like that."

Nadzia stepped inside the cottage, making note of the open

wooden shelving, the stack of quilts, the herbs hanging from the rafters. Cozy. Hopefully welcoming.

"How nice," Petronela said. "It's...sparkly in here."

"Effect of the mountain air. Early ice crystals," said Esmerelda quickly. "Tea?"

Esmerelda poured their cups while Nadzia shoved biscuits in Petronela's direction. She didn't remember Esmerelda making these earlier. She must have baked them while she was escorting Janosik home.

At their rapid explanations, Petronela blinked, looking back and forth between them.

"We don't get many visitors," Nadzia explained. "I'm sorry if we appear too eager. We're...I'm just excited. Our nearest neighbor is over in the next valley and he's a hermit. Doesn't like company."

"You're fine. I feel quite welcome. Besides, I don't do much visiting anymore, so this is nice." Petronela took a biscuit. "My aunt and cousins love to go calling on people and having folks to our house, but I prefer serving and staying out of their way." She looked back outside. "I don't have a dog to help with the sheep. May we continue our visit outside? I don't trust the sheep to not wander off."

"Yes. And I could show you our goat." Nadzia grinned. She wanted to speak privately anyway, as girls do. Or, at least the girls in books she'd read. She wanted a friend so badly. Even one who she only saw a few times a year.

"Of course. I was looking for the goat when you found me."

"WHAT TO DO, WHAT TO DO?" Esmerelda muttered while she observed from the window. The girl was clearly underfed and overworked, as were many of the people in town. The war had been hard on them, but for some it was harder. That dress she wore was thin and patched too many times to be proper. But she was proud, as evidenced when Nadzia insisted the girl borrow a jacket and hat when they went outside. She wouldn't readily take charity.

We could keep her. It was almost as if Nadzia was there whispering in her ear. Nadzia had a habit of picking up strays, but normally they were forest creatures, not a girl.

While she mused, she pulled out her wand and waved it over the garden basket. A sparkly cloud billowed and swirled as half the turnips and squash rose and danced their way to the root cellar at the back of the cottage. A separate stack of green beans and legumes lined up by the sink. And *zip, zap,* canned jars appeared on the shelves.

Esmerelda went to the window to see how the girls were getting on when a movement across the meadow caught her eye.

"Oh, what is this?" she picked up the latest kitten and showed him the view outside the window of a young man trotting down the path. *If my eyes don't deceive me, that's the young prince. And the plot thickens.*

CHAPTER 14

"*T*his is Olenka, my naughty sheep," said Petronela. She gently tugged its pink ear and it shook its head before skittering away. "Always straying from the others. I have to keep my eye on her."

"She's cute."

"That's why she gets away with so much. I know she doesn't mean to wander. She's a sheep after all. It's my responsibility to guide her."

"Esmerelda kept sheep for a few years but they vexed her too much. She sold them to a shepherd across—" Nadzia paused midsentence as her gaze caught another person climbing their mountain today. A young male variety, wearing baggy cotton pants, a mountain shirt rolled up to the elbows, and a shepherd's hat.

"What is it?" Petronela asked, turning around. She took a step back to be in line with Nadzia.

"A boy," Nadzia whispered.

Petronela squinted. "Not just a boy. A prince. That's the youngest son of the king. Not that you could tell based on his clothing." She leaned forward. "I haven't seen him in years. Wonder what brings him up here?"

Nadzia reached over and squeezed Petronela's hand. "You know him? What should we do?"

Petronela laughed. "We could wait until he gets closer and then talk to him."

"Of course." Nadzia smoothed her skirt. What a busy day on the mountain.

The prince looked like he was trying to pretend he hadn't seen them, keeping his gaze on the path, his head slightly tilted away from them. Petronela seemed to find this amusing and when he got close enough, she called out to him by name.

Startled, he stopped and stared.

When his face didn't register recognition, Petronela's teasing smile dimmed. "He doesn't know me," she whispered, looking down at her tattered dress. She let out a breath.

Nadzia's heart sank. *Petronela didn't know how much she'd changed until now.* Nadzia tried to stick up for her new friend. "He's probably too far away and obviously not expecting you to be up here. Wait until he gets closer."

"You're right. Besides, he's always been on the shy side." She lifted her chin as she waited, but her expression belied her hurt feelings.

The mountain path came near the cottage, close enough that the prince would have to go out of his way to show the girls he hadn't seen or heard them, especially when Petronela's sheep wandered his way and blocked the path so he had to come closer.

He nodded at them as he tried to skirt around Olenka.

Petronela was the first to speak. "Nadzia," she said, "Have you met the prince, Marek?"

"Hi," Nadzia smiled, then looked away. Here was a prince. In her meadow. Shouldn't she curtsy, or something? The girls in books always curtsied. But Petronela didn't, so she didn't either.

"You know who I am?" He looked shocked and sounded disappointed.

Petronela frowned. "Shouldn't we know who you are?"

"I'm in disguise," he said. "Some chaps and I were going over the mountains to find out if the peace treaty still holds. I gave up waiting for them and thought I'd go on my own."

"And what do you expect to find?" Petronela nudged Olenka off the path.

"Hopefully nothing. I'll look for weapons stockpiles and the like. My hope is that I can report back that our kingdom is safe."

"Isn't that a job for the general?"

"Yes, but." He stopped, his cheeks turning red. "They have a new plan to ensure lasting peace, but I think it's tenuous at best."

"What is the new plan?"

He turned redder, if that were possible. Then he opened his eyes wide as he looked at Petronela. "I remember you. You'd come up to the castle with your father. You're the girl who liked to play hide and seek and were impossible to find. Little Nela."

Petronela rose up on her toes, seemingly pleased he remembered who she used to be. "I was rather good. The secret is in being still. You might want to consider that if you continue with your plans."

"And patient. Most children would get bored and make a noise so I could find them. Didn't you want to be found?"

"That wasn't the purpose of the game."

"Where are you living now, if you don't mind my asking?"

"Still at our family home. My aunt and cousins live there with me." She looked uncomfortable. "Now you've gone and changed the subject. Back on course. What is the general's plan that has you flustered?"

"A marriage. To one of the Burgosov girls, a prominent family over the mountain. The general thinks that if our families are joined, their kingdom would be less likely to attack us again."

"Or more likely, since they'll have one foot in the house."

Marek raised his hands. "Exactly. That's what I tried to tell them. Wish your father was still around to back me up." He smacked his forehead. "Oh, I'm sorry. That was insensitive of me."

"It's fine. I wish he were still around to back me up, too." Petronela bit her lip. "But never mind me, your situation appears more dire."

"There's not much I can do. My life is not my own, and I have to think about the good of the kingdom."

"Both your situations are dire," said Nadzia. "Why don't you stay here in the mountains and live your lives free?" Even as she said it, she realized her idea would never work and made her sound terribly young.

"Sweet thing, that is kind of you," said Petronela, "But hiding out won't solve my problems. Nor will Marek solve his that way."

"Even so, you may come up here any time you want," Nadzia said. "You're always welcome."

"Thank you." Petronela squeezed Nadzia's arm. Then a smile spread across her face and she turned to the prince. "You were planning on spying on the Burgosov girls, weren't you? To see what they're like."

"And look for stockpiles." He grinned. "Don't forget the stockpiles."

The two stood there, smiling at each other for several moments, and Nadzia sensed she was intruding on some intimacy she didn't understand. They were standing there, all three, but Petronela and Marek were two together.

"Come talk to Esmerelda," Nadzia said. "She's got a knack for knowing what to do."

CHAPTER 15

*I*nside the mountain cottage, the small table had been spread for tea again, this time with finger sandwiches, additional biscuits, and lumps of sugar in a bowl. Nadzia could have sworn none of those items had been in the cottage not ten minutes ago. Maybe Janosik had left them behind without her seeing.

"Hungry?" Esmerelda asked as the trio stepped through the doorway.

Nadzia and Petronela exchanged bemused glances before sitting down at the table again, while Esmerelda fawned over the prince. "People work up an appetite climbing this hill," she said, shoving more food in his direction. "You need your strength."

Over tea, they presented the case before Esmerelda, who nodded silently all the while.

"I know of those girls. Is it a happy marriage you are wanting?"

Marek nodded.

"Best keep the mountain between you, then. One will nag to the bone and the other will spend your money faster than, well, faster than a country at war."

"I thought as much. But what am I to do? Father is set on peace, and mother is set on grandchildren. Soon."

Petronela and Nadzia exchanged a look.

"Wives can be persuasive," Esmerelda said. "What if you talked to your mother and offered an alternative. A local girl to strengthen the loyalty within our own kingdom. Not a princess from another realm, but instead, elevate the young women here. Any of them could become a princess."

Marek glanced at Petronela. "Any of them?"

"Your kingdom is still struggling from this recent war." Esmerelda filled his tea cup. "Hope will go a long way to recovery. If the people knew how committed your family was to them, they would get over their anger faster."

"You think they're angry?" Marek reached for another biscuit.

"Mostly tired," said Petronela. "We wanted to keep our freedom, but the cost was high."

Marek's shoulders dropped. "If I give up my freedom at a high cost and marry a Burgosov, then won't that show the people I suffer with them?"

"No, if you suffer, we'll suffer more with you," Petronela said. "I'm afraid that if you let one Burgosov move in, the rest will follow and we'll be overtaken. We're a small kingdom compared to theirs. Based on past actions, they won't respect our sovereignty, and we'll be made nothing more than their military outpost or vacation land."

"They do like our cheese," said Nadzia.

Marek and Petronela burst out laughing.

Nadzia blushed. "They do. We have a peddler that comes by in the fall and spring to buy oscypki from us—says our patterns are the best. He brings it back over the mountains. Once before the snow falls and again as soon as the pass has cleared. He came through this morning on his way back home."

"There is hope for the neighboring kingdom, yet," said Marek. He stood as if to go. "Thank you for your insightful words, babuszka. I'll think about what you've said. Seems my spying plans have yielded fruit after all, and the company was much more enjoyable than I had anticipated." He nodded at the group, his eyes lingering on Petronela.

He likes her! Nadzia glanced at Petronela for her reaction.

"May I walk you back to town?" Marek said.

Petronela's face lit up. "That would be lovely."

She likes him, too.

"I'll go gather your sheep," he said, and left the cottage.

Petronela stayed behind to help clear the table. When she reached out to take the teapot, Esmerelda wrapped her hand around the girl's. Bruises lined Petronela's tender inner arm.

Nadzia stifled a gasp. What had happened to her?

Esmerelda met Petronela's gaze. "You don't have to go back. You can stay here."

Petronela lowered her eyes. "It's fine. Looks worse than it feels."

"Why don't you leave? You can come live with us. We'll treat you well."

"Memories of my parents are all I have left, and they are strongest in the house. I can't walk away from those feelings. Not yet."

Marek poked his head back in the door and Petronela slid her sleeves down.

"You ready?" he asked. "The sun is already behind the mountain."

She handed the teapot to Esmerelda. "Thank you for your kindness. Hopefully we can visit again, soon."

"Remember your herbs," Esmerelda said. She nodded toward the sideboard.

Nadzia turned and saw a small basket filled with a variety of fresh green herbs. She handed the basket to Petronela.

"I'd almost forgotten my purpose in coming here," Petronela said. "Can't imagine what I would have done if I'd gotten halfway home and remembered." She pulled out her coins, and when Esmerelda refused them, she left them on the table.

"The young often get distracted," Esmerelda said, her gaze leading them all to look out the door where Marek stood waiting.

Petronela cleared her throat. "Yes, well, I better go. Thanks again. For everything."

Nadzia leaned on the door post watching them go. Little work had gotten done today, but she'd strengthened several friendships.

"You look contented," said Esmerelda.

"I am. It's nice having visitors."

"What am I to do with you, girl?" asked Esmerelda. "You were only given to me for a time, and that time has been longer than I thought."

"What do you mean?"

"You've been a blessing for sure, but it's time we look to your future." Esmerelda watched Petronela herding her three sheep back down the path to town.

Nadzia rested her head against her mother's shoulder. "My future is with you. I see how you rub your knuckles, how slowly you get out of bed in the morning. You've raised me well, and it's my turn to take care of you. I can cook and clean and sell your herbs to buy the things you can't make."

"I'm not as bad off as you think. I may outlive you even though I look older than the hills."

"Is that so?" Nadzia turned away from the door, bemused at Esmerelda's bragging. "Is there anything else I need to know about you?"

Esmerelda shrugged. "A woman should always keep a little mystery about her."

CHAPTER 16

Several weeks later, Petronela eagerly herded the sheep up into the mountains again. She'd made a big show in front of her stepmother about not wanting to go—the path was steep; the air was cold—she wanted to ensure no one else considered coming with her or going in her stead.

As soon as she was out of sight of the house, Petronela hustled the sheep along. These trips to the mountain cottage had become her delight. What would her cousins do if they learned the prince often visited the cottage in the mountains, too? All their private tutoring lessons were meant to help them marry up in the world and who was higher up than the prince? Even Petronela would be intimidated by him and his position if she hadn't already met him when they were younger.

The walk up the mountain gave her time to think. Her home situation couldn't stay the way it was. She was slowly dying in that house and she knew it. Her time in the mountains made her realize how resigned she had become. Her father, though he thought he was doing what was best for her when he remarried, wouldn't want her to give up to the enemy. He'd want her to fight.

The strain of walking up the mountain had made her physically stronger, especially with Esmerelda's hearty food waiting for her. Her legs rarely tired now, and she was no longer gasping for breath by the time she'd gotten to the meadow.

But the fellowship up the mountain, that was the best of all. It fed the soul. She was too shy to admit it to Esmerelda and Nadzia, but she was already beginning to think of them as her family.

Then there was Marek. How exactly did she feel about him?

The last time she saw him, they'd parted ways in the marketplace. Marek was silent and serious about his plans, and Petronela's sheep caused such a ruckus that the goodbye was unsatisfying. She'd chased Olenka, that naughty sheep, and when she looked up, Marek was gone, absorbed into the crowd.

It had been surprisingly welcome to reconnect with someone from her life before her father had died. Such warm memories, and she hoped Marek felt the same.

At the very least, she knew he could relate to her pain. After his brother died, he'd retreated into the castle. Back then, she didn't understand why his grieving took so long, but now that she'd experienced loss herself, she had a better idea. Of course, rumors were that his pain cut deep because he blamed himself for his brother's death, no matter how unfair the charge. Friends can tell someone it wasn't their fault, but if they chose to keep believing it, one couldn't change their mind. It was something he'd have to work out on his own.

For Petronela, life after her father died had become such drudgery, but little victories like new friends and renewed acquaintances helped. They were reminders that life was always changing and her future was malleable.

Her cousins wouldn't always live in the house, especially the way her aunt was so focused on training them for "positions of influence," whatever that meant. After that, it would be Petronela's turn.

Meanwhile, she had a place to escape to. Friends to meet. She picked up the pace, eager to get there.

Nadzia waited outside the cottage and waved enthusiastically when Petronela rounded the bend.

Petronela smiled and waved back. The sheep, familiar with the routine, headed for the bits of green persisting to grow despite the cold weather.

"So, has Marek been up here lately?" Petronela asked after giving Nadzia a hug.

Nadzia laughed, pure joy rolling off her.

"You two should quit pretending to bump into each other here and plan it already."

"What do you mean?" *Are my thoughts so easy to read?*

"Esmerelda and I see right through you. Both of you act like this meadow is the town square, and 'fancy meeting you here' when you both come here looking for each other."

Petronela smiled. Nadzia had such a gentle innocence about her; she'd be happy to find her new friends in love. *If* they were in love. She'd not rest on it until she knew for sure. "You think he looks for me?"

"He makes the trip every day, which is more than I can say for you. So, yes, he's pretty determined to see you."

Petronela bit her lips to rein in her smile. He'd not let on that he'd come every day, but he had given her hints of his feelings. He'd held her gaze. Brushed his hands against hers while they were walking. Brought his sheepdog with him to help her corral the sheep so they could talk more earnestly on their walks.

"Every day, you say?" she asked later, after Esmerelda had filled her with mushroom soup and rye bread. The conversation was welcoming, but Petronela couldn't hide who she was hoping to see.

Nadzia frowned. "He has been. Something must have kept him today."

"This week he was going to talk to his family about what they thought of him marrying a local girl instead of one of the Burgosov girls," Petronela said quietly.

Nadzia and Esmerelda exchanged a look. They smiled.

"I knew it," Nadzia said.

Petronela laughed at her exuberance. "But he's not here today. What if his parents have forbidden him from seeing me? When my father was alive, they may have approved, but not now with my family in ruin." Petronela trailed off, not finishing the thought.

"Oh, child. Don't think like that."

But Petronela wasn't swayed by Esmerelda's rebuke. She couldn't fully let go of her heart until she knew what he was going to do. Marek had told her the pressure he was under to marry for the alliance. Given the guilt he still carried about letting his family down, he just might reverse course and marry one of the Burgosov girls.

During one of their intense conversations walking back to town, Marek had told her how the accident still haunted him. The devastating avalanche in which his brother sacrificed his life for Marek's replayed in his mind over and over. He said he couldn't help thinking that if his brother had still been alive, he would be the one having to marry a Burgosov. It was one of the main reasons he had ever considered the sacrifice. For the kingdom and for his brother's memory.

"You think your brother would be honored by you marrying across the mountain?" she'd said. "Seems to me he'd rather you learn how to lead your own country your own way."

He hadn't answered. Instead, he'd turned the subject around to her.

"Shouldn't you be bringing the sheep down the mountain this time of year instead of up higher? All the shepherds are abandoning their wooden shacks in preparation for the winter," Marek said.

"Yes, but my stepmother insists."

"Seems to me like she insists on a lot of things," he'd said.

She'd not answered and they'd continued the walk in uneasy silence.

From Petronela's perspective they both had family problems they needed to work out. They would be stronger as one, but first they needed to find a way to be together.

CHAPTER 17

*P*etronela spent the next few days with her gaze constantly wandering to the stone castle.

What was happening up there?

The people in the marketplace carried about their business like the castle didn't exist. Like their futures weren't being decided. The jam woman continued to sell out of her jams. The chandler added a fresh batch of tallow candles to his window display. The children darted in and around the daily shoppers without a care. "Excuse me, miss," said a polite one after he'd bumped into her.

She was aching to know how well the talk with Marek and his parents was going. From what Petronela remembered, Marek's mother was elegant, removed, but also kind. She'd served Petronela peach *kompot* one long evening when her father had brought her to a party. Petronela, Marek, and his brother had been the only children, and maybe that was why the queen herself had served her. That had been the last party she'd ever gone to at the castle. The parties had stopped not long after because that's the year the accident had happened.

The town crier blasted his bugle, shocking her out of her

reverie. Those closest to him covered their ears, while the chicken seller grabbed and held his squawking hen. The blacksmith ceased his clanking and the shoppers all stopped their haggling and hushed their children to hear what he had to say. It wasn't often the crier came to town and when he did it was oft to deliver bad news.

Petronela leaned in, her heart fluttering with worry.

"In celebration of peace, and with a look to the future, there will be a ball," said the crier. "All the young ladies of the land are invited to the castle to meet and dance with the eligible prince who is looking for a suitable bride from among his own kingdom, his own people."

Petronela stared up at the castle. Was this good news for her or not? It meant they'd agreed to not force the Burgosov marriage. But they'd not agreed to herself? Is that why he didn't come to the mountain?

At the end of his short speech, the crier tacked a notice to the information tree and set off, presumably for the next town. Mothers with daughters of marriageable age flocked to the notice and talk of ball gowns and hairstyles began in earnest.

Petronela turned away.

A chance to wed the prince…the lessons the cousins have been getting. Her aunt would surely try to thrust her daughters on Marek. All the mothers would be looking for a way for their daughters to shine in front of the king and queen. Where did that leave her? She needed to talk to Marek to find out what was going on.

"A ball," exclaimed one of the elderly women knitting on a bench by the fountain. "Like in the old days."

"Would that we were young again," said her friend. "Remember the ball we went to when you met your Florek? He was so nervous you were watching that he forgot the steps to the *zbójnicki* and started improvising." The two elbowed each other and laughed.

Seeing Petronela watching them, the first said, "Be sure you go, young lady. If for nothing else than the memories."

Petronela nodded and continued on her way. She would love to go, but what would she wear to a ball? When she was younger, she had closets bursting with pretty dresses, the traditional mountain dresses with colorful embroidered flowers, but Marzena sold everything of worth after Father died.

Then when the soldiers left the estate, Marzena moved them all back in. She had always been jealous of that house. Petronela remembered her mother telling Papa what a hard time her sister was giving her for living in such an extravagant home. But at the first opportunity, Marzena moved in, rummaged through all the closets, and got rid of all Mama's favorite and precious things. "Your mother always had poor taste," she said, taking down the silk curtains.

Even if father were alive and came home from the war, he would think he'd walked into the wrong house. With Marzena's tables and chairs and carpets and paintings, it was as if Marzena were trying to erase every evidence of Mama. By the way her stepmother looked at Petronela, it was a wonder she was even allowed to stay in her own house.

Maybe that's why Petronela made herself so useful. Marzena might be stubborn, but so was Petronela. She could outlast her stepsisters, see them go off and get married. Maybe the same would happen with Marzena and they would all one day leave and Petronela could put everything back to rights.

She had been able to squirrel away a few select family heirlooms, hidden in a trunk underneath worn baby and childhood items that were of no value to anyone else and therefore couldn't be sold. The trunk! That was it. It hid the one dress of Mother's that Petronela was able to pack away. It was terribly old-fashioned now, but it was the one Mama was wearing when she met Papa. A plain silver dress with no adornments. But it was better than the rags she was wearing now. And the cousins wouldn't even get jealous over it because it was so out-of-date and they only wore the latest fashions.

With a lighter step, Petronela let herself daydream all the way home.

LATER THAT DAY, the tutor arrived, and after leading him into the sitting room, Petronela slipped into the kitchen to get tea. She'd whip through all her chores and then take a closer look at that dress. She put the plates on a tray, added the cups and the teapot. Last minute, she added almond biscuits, Jolanta's favorite. Maybe it would put them in a good mood.

She carried the heavy tray, walking slowly to keep the cups from rattling. Marzena hated that sound, and today was not the day to irritate her.

The door was open ajar and the tutor's voice floated out. "The Burgosovs would be most generous to you and your girls if they —" His voice got quiet and Petronela stopped.

What business did Marzena have with the Burgosovs?

She leaned in and the dishes rattled. Before she had time to step back and pretend she'd just gotten there, Aunt Marzena stepped into the hall.

"Eavesdropping?"

"No, just adjusting the tray. I made sure the tea pot was filled to the top. You said last time you ran out?"

Petronela forced a smile. Marzena's exact words had been "I've never met a more incompetent servant in my life." Her aunt didn't know the half of it. When it came to taking care of the house, she did so without complaint and with an almost reverent attitude toward her former life, her Mama, and her Papa. But when it came to serving her ungrateful and selfish family, she did what was necessary and nothing more. She was never mean, nor did she play tricks or do other things she'd heard other servants talk about. She just never wasted her efforts if she didn't need to. Pearls before swine and all.

Petronela set the tray down and turned to leave, but the tutor stopped her.

"Stay for a moment. We need another dance partner."

"Oh, she knows nothing," said Marzena. "She'll be no help."

"Will you dance with Jolanta then?" he asked Marzena pointedly.

Marzena waved her hand. "Very well then. The servant girl can help. Jolanta's stepped on my toes enough for one day."

The tutor nodded and motioned for Petronela to join them.

She shook her head. "No, I couldn't possibly," she said. She didn't like anything about that man and didn't want to get any closer.

"Oh here," said Jolanta, grabbing Petronela. "I don't know why they're making such a fuss. You just go like this." Jolanta proceeded to bounce around the room, soundly stepping on Petronela's feet every time she got the chance. "It's fun, isn't it?" she said.

Wincing, Petronela nodded. "It could be." It was fun when she and Nadzia practiced in the mountain cottage. Esmerelda knew the traditional dances and they were a fun way to pass the time when it was raining.

"Well, you'll never know," said Hortensia. "It's not like you'll be going to the ball."

"Why not? Everyone is invited."

"Yes, but you've nothing to wear."

"I may not have the prettiest dress, but I'll manage."

"You hear that, Mother?" asked Hortensia. "Cinderella thinks she can go to the ball."

"Our little bird? Why, she'll be too busy picking the rocks out of the lentils. We'll need our nourishment after a long night of dancing."

The doorbell rang, stopping the family from their verbal

assault. Petronela gladly excused herself to go open the front door. It was a delivery boy carrying a large box. An unmistakable box from the premier dressmaker in the village.

"Petronela?" The delivery boy read off the form.

"Thank you," she said, but before she could reach for it, Marzena stepped in between her and the delivery.

"You? Did you steal from the household funds to buy yourself a dress? Let's see it then." She took the box from the baffled boy.

"I didn't order anything." Though she had a good idea who did, and it warmed her heart to know he was thinking of her. He did want her at the ball after all.

"Are you sure it's for Petronela?" said Hortensia to the delivery boy who was trying to escape off the porch.

He showed her the form. "Says so right here."

"Hmph."

They all followed Marzena back into the sitting room where she proceeded to open the box. Inside lay a traditional mountain gown, ivory wool with embroidered crimson and pink poppies outlined with golden threads that glimmered in the light.

Hortensia gasped.

Marzena's gaze bore into hers. "*How dare you.* A gown like this would feed the household for six months."

"I didn't." It was all Petronela could do to convince her.

"I'll hold onto it until we get to the truth. Perhaps we can take it back and exchange it for two new dresses for my girls. A reward for them studying so diligently." She smiled in a way that made Petronela's blood run cold.

The tutor stood near the fireplace, his calculating gaze taking everything in.

Marzena, Hortensia, Jolanta. The way they were all staring at her...she lived as a stranger in their midst, the home of her childhood.

Petronela cared more about the kitchen door that stuck in rainy weather than she cared about her aunt, now stepmother, and about the squeaky floor more than her cousins, now stepsisters.

She balled her hands into fists. No matter what obstacles Marzena threw at her, it wouldn't matter. Marek had given her the means to escape. His personal invitation meant he'd found a way, she was sure of it.

"Oops, silly me." Hortensia held up her hands in a helpless gesture and frowned. A bottle was in her right hand.

Jolanta raced over to the dress and covered her mouth with her hands. Her wide eyes waited for Petronela's reaction.

A blotch of black ink had stained the ivory part of the bodice. Not even the cleverest alterations could fix it. Of all Hortensia's cruelty over the years, this cut deep. Petronela couldn't stay in this house any longer. She needed to leave, but not without her greatest treasure.

Careful to show no emotion, Petronela turned and walked out the front door.

"Where is she going?" Jolanta asked.

They would find out soon enough. Petronela marched straight to the barn, pocketed a metal chisel from the work bench, then located the ladder. She hefted the unwieldy thing back to the house amidst the curious stares of her family and the tutor. She was leaving, that's what she was doing.

After setting up the ladder near the front door, she climbed it and began working the stained-glass window loose. Somehow, she'd get it out, even if she had to take a hammer to the wall. They could have everything else. She'd walk away from her inheritance with just the window.

"Stop that." Aunt Marzena's sharp voice rose above the speculative whispers of her children.

"It's all I want," Petronela said. "You win. Keep the house. Keep the land. I don't want any of it. I'll just take this one thing and be on my way." It would be hard to carry such a heavy leaded window all the way up to the cottage, but she was prepared to take all night if need be. She had to get away. As she worked the wood, some of the frame began to break away. Father was nothing if not thorough. He'd meant for this window to stay above the door forever.

"Not one more move or I'll have you arrested for theft," Aunt Marzena gestured to the tutor. "Isn't that right? I've got witnesses. Besides, everyone knows that window belongs to the house and therefore to me."

Petronela hesitated, her gaze fixed on the beautiful glass tree. She had no doubt her aunt would do exactly as she said. But could the prince legally intervene on her behalf?

"Come down this instant before you do any more damage."

Petronela hated to back down now, but since the surge of adrenaline had subsided, she had begun to think more clearly again. She wouldn't allow them to push her to make a rash decision. It wouldn't be much longer. Once her future was secured, she could come back here and demand the window. It was more than generous for her to let go of everything else that should be her inheritance. With the support of the royal family, Petronela would have the power to force Marzena to relent.

Petronela reluctantly put the chisel in her pocket. For a moment there she'd been exhilarated, finally able to show what she really thought of her family. That she cared for them as little as they cared for her.

As she packed up the ladder, her rage simmered. How could Hortensia be so cruel? Again and again, these women revealed themselves to be mean and spiteful. But above all else, Petronela felt pity. Pity that Hortensia was so petty that she thought she might win by spoiling the dress. It was only a ruined dress. Marek would understand, and her nasty cousins could feel like they'd won. For a time.

CHAPTER 18

The day of the ball began with Marzena handing Petronela a long list of chores, from her regular tasks, to helping Hortensia and Jolanta get ready for the ball, to continuing to prepare the house for winter.

"I don't know why these chores must be done today," she said, glancing at the list Marzena handed her at breakfast. *Clean gutters, repaper the cupboards, inventory the toolshed.*

"Don't talk back, child. Winter always sneaks up on us in the mountains."

"And we don't want you at the ball." Jolanta coughed as her sister elbowed her in the ribs. "What?" she said.

Not a problem. Petronela had never been so motivated. Even though she hadn't seen Marek since the announcement, his gift was enough to tell her everything she needed to know. Tonight was going to change the course of her life. Nothing her family said or did to her would bring her down.

Hortensia smiled smugly. "We'll look beautiful in our new gowns."

Petronela looked up sharply from her list. "What new gowns?"

"Our tutor was so thrilled with our progress he said he wanted to invest in our futures," Jolanta said.

"He bought us each a gown. Too bad you didn't agree to be tutored." Hortensia smiled smugly at her mother.

Beside the fact tutoring was never offered to her, Petronela wouldn't have submitted to the teaching anyway. "The invitation didn't say you could only come wearing a new dress."

Hortensia and Jolanta exchanged uneasy looks.

"Then I suppose if you get your work done, you can go." Marzena spoke the words to Petronela, but her gaze was fixed on her daughters.

"I'm always done by evening," Petronela said, watching a silent conversation go on between her cousins and stepmother. Her insides tensed.

"Yes, but this is the start of winter. Before the snow comes there is so much that needs to be done. You still have food left in the garden, do you not?"

"Only the cabbage—"

"Which need to come out now. And the squash?"

"Fine." It wasn't impossible. They were just being difficult was all. Petronela gritted her teeth. She'd show them. They had no idea how much time it took to do any of the chores as they never did any themselves.

"Oh, look. It's almost time to go." Marzena stood in front of the grandfather clock in the hall. "Are the girls finished yet?"

Petronela wiped her hand across her brow before sticking the final pin into Jolanta's fancy hairdo. "Done. Give me one moment and I'll be ready to go." She'd hoped for time for a bath, but at this point, she'd settle for getting ready in time to drive with her relatives. It was too late for her to get to the castle on her own. By the time she walked, it would be over and Marek would think she'd not wanted to attend.

Hortensia laughed. "I'm not waiting. The prince's dance card will be filled if we get there late."

"You still have to bring the carriage around. I'll be ready."

Petronela raced to her room and shoved a chair under the handle to lock it. Then she released the hidden door into the passageway where she'd hidden the trunk filled with her mother's belongings. She'd stacked the top with personalized baby things Marzena wouldn't be able to sell. No one would buy a baby blanket stitched with her name, or handkerchiefs with her initials. Buried at the very bottom was her mother's silver dress made out of pale gray silk and laced with silver thread. Petronela had grown enough that she hoped it would fit with minimal adjustments. There'd been no time to try it on or air it out. For her plan to work, her family couldn't know anything about it until there was no time for them to intervene.

She put it on and quickly sneaked into Marzena's room to see what she looked like in the full mirror. Her breath caught at what she saw. The mirror was angled so her reflection started with the tip of her nose and on down. If she hadn't known she was the one standing there, she would have sworn it was her mother. The gown was constructed with a simple crisscross bodice and full skirt, but it wasn't plain. Old-fashioned, but also timeless.

"What are you doing in my room?"

Petronela jumped at the sharpness of Marzena's voice. That woman ruined every moment. Petronela wiped her eyes before turning around. "I didn't think you'd mind terribly if I checked that my dress fit."

"I do mind. Terribly."

The cousins, sensing trouble, scrambled in behind. "What's she doing?"

"Apparently she thinks she's going to a ball," Marzena said. "Dressed as her mother."

Petronela took a deep breath. "By royal decree I'm going to a ball." Not even her aunt would go against a royal decree.

"You're going to wear that?" Hortensia's sneer said it all. "You can't let her go, Mama. She'll ruin everything." Hortensia reached out and pulled the sleeve until it tore.

Petronela twisted away before she could do more damage.

"You can't be with the prince." Jolanta darted forward. "You're cursed. Everyone you love dies."

She said it like it was as obvious and real as the blue sky.

"First your mother. Then your father. Even our papa died after you visited us."

Petronela took a step away, stung anew by the increased cruelty. Aunt Marzena stood with her shoulders back, her chin up and looked down her nose with a steely gaze.

This is what they thought of her? This is why they punished her?

"I'm not cursed."

"It's true," Hortensia added unhelpfully. "Hasn't anyone pointed it out to you yet? We don't even want to live with you, but Mama says we have to." Hortensia nodded to her sister and Jolanta ripped the other sleeve clear off in her exuberance to impress her sister.

Tears stung in Petronela's eyes. The delicate silk split not at the seam, but at a weak place in the fabric, leaving a jagged edge. Even if she had time to sew it, it wouldn't look right. She couldn't wear this dress. Now she really did have nothing to wear. Not to meet Marek's parents. Not when she needed to be presentable in front of the whole kingdom.

"Pity. But you can't go dressed like that," said Aunt Marzena

"No, I can't." Her voice came out so quiet, like it belonged to someone else. What was she going to do? Even if she fixed the tears and found a way to cover them up with a wrap she still couldn't get to the castle on time.

"Bye, Cinderella! Keep the fires burning for us." Hortensia waved as she scurried out the door with Jolanta at her heels.

Jolanta stuck her tongue out and slammed the door. The thud reverberated in the foyer and the stained-glass window jerked from its frame and began to tilt precariously outward.

Petronela gasped. Her first instinct was to stand under it to try to catch it, but quickly realizing the foolishness of that, jumped up the stairs to safety.

The window fell and crashed onto the hard tiles, smashing into jagged pieces.

"No." She put her hands to her face in shock. She shook her head. The strongest connection she had to her mother and father was gone in an instant. Her stepfamily took even that from her. Petronela began to shake with rage.

She carefully picked her way to the door. She would not hold back when she yelled at Jolanta and made her see the damage she caused. But the carriage was already driving down the road.

Petronela stood at the open door, dumbfounded, until her legs collapsed. She was tired. Bone tired. She'd worked twice as hard, filled with hope, and now had nothing to show for it.

"I give up. They win. Their mean, spiteful, jealous selves win."

CHAPTER 19

*I*nstead of yelling out her frustration, Petronela cried into the floor by the open door, clutching the torn sleeve, surrounded by the shattered glass. "I'm sorry Papa. Mama. I'm not strong. You've left me alone in this world and I am undone."

A gust of wind blew her hair and made her tears cold on her cheeks.

"No, dearie. You are giving up much too soon."

Petronela lifted her eyes to stare at two brown boots standing outside her door. She followed them up to a mountain dress worn by a plump figure with kind eyes and white hair.

"Esmerelda! Where did you come from?"

Petronela blinked as she tried to make sense of a pretty pair of fairy wings sprouting out of Esmerelda's back, glittering in the moonlight. The wings had to be an illusion from the cold air and her tears. She rubbed her eyes.

"You've no time to waste. The ball is about to begin, and you'll be fashionably late, just like the king and queen, if we get started now."

"What are you talking about? Why are you here?"

"You are a girl in need of some help. I suspected as much from the moment I first saw you. Why would your stepfamily risk you getting ahead of them?"

"What do you mean?"

"Oh, dearie. Your innocence is part of your charm, but sometimes you have to pay more attention to what's going on around you."

Petronela frowned. "But I do. My cousins are up to something with the Burgosovs across the mountain. I just haven't figured out what, yet."

By Esmerelda's expression, Petronela could tell the mountain woman knew something, and she wasn't pleased. There it was again. A glimmer of a wing. Petronela tilted her head. "The way the light is hitting the cold air...the fog...it looks like you've got wings."

Esmerelda smiled. "I do. I'm your fairy godmother. I only reveal my wings when there's a need."

Petronela gaped. "But those are stories. Fairies aren't real." She'd outgrown fairies the day her papa died.

"That's why I reveal my wings. It helps with my credibility."

"Where's Nadzia? Is she a fairy, too?"

"No. You know her story. She was left on my doorstep." Esmerelda rolled up her sleeves. "Can we get down to business? The ball will be over before we get through the basics here. You *do* want to go?"

"Yes, of course."

"Then get me something I can use for a carriage. That castle is a ways off."

"They've already taken our old horses."

"Do what I ask, and you'll see the power of a fairy godmother. Do you have a garden?"

"There's not much in it. I had to empty it before I could go to the ball, but I left a few things out there for the animals to scavenge. Aunt Marzena never goes back there, so the far corner still has some of the late fall vegetables. Are you hungry? I can fix you something from the food in the kitchen."

Esmerelda shook her head. "I need a fresh pumpkin. They last longer."

Petronela led the way to the garden. "There might be one under here somewhere. There are a lot of leaves and vines, so one could be hiding." Sure enough, she'd missed a small one.

"Don't cut it off," Esmerelda said. I'll use the vine, too." She pulled out a silver wand and waved it over the pumpkin. Sparkles fell like ice crystals and when they landed on the pumpkin the orange ball began to grow and grow and turned to gold. The vines grew with it, forming a frame and wheels until what stood before them was a golden carriage as fancy as any the king owned.

"That's. Well. That's…" Petronela smiled. "Marvelous."

Esmerelda grinned. "Never get tired of it. Got any mice?"

This time Petronela didn't hesitate. "Marzena hates them. She's got box traps all over, but I always let them out into the fields." She ran to check her traps and found two little mice in the kitchen waiting to be freed. She brought these to Esmerelda where she waited in the driveway.

In no time at all, Esmerelda had completed the retinue. Two magnificent white horses joined the golden carriage, which was also outfitted with smart-looking footmen, standing at attention.

"There you go." Esmerelda surveyed her creation with pleasure.

Petronela still couldn't believe what she was witnessing. Who knew unassuming Esmerelda wielded such power? But there was one more thing Petronela would need. She shivered in the cold, indicating her torn dress. "What about this?"

"The best part." Esmerelda closed her eyes and looped her wand in the air.

Soon, Petronela was encased in glittery magic. She watched in wonder as her simple dress transformed into a ball gown in pale gold to match the carriage. The torn sleeve in her hand grew to become a wrap which would keep her shoulders warm going to and from the ball. Nadzia's tatting pattern covered the fabric.

"Oh, Esmerelda!" Crimson, orange, and gold poppies embroidered themselves as she watched, adding a dash of color climbing a thin green vine up the skirt. The dress had become a mix of her mother's gown and Marek's gift, gold from Esmerelda and lace from Nadzia.

"I don't know what to say. It's perfect. I couldn't have dreamed of anything so lovely."

Esmerelda grinned, pleased at Nela's response. She leaned in to examine her handiwork. "Also, I added a little something extra to this one. Pay attention to those around you. Your dress will help you decide whose intentions are pure."

Petronela took a step and her bare toes poked out from under the skirt.

"Almost forgot your shoes," Esmerelda said as she pulled from the broken stained-glass window, shaping glass shoes to match Petronela's feet. Then she dropped delicate diamonds into the dancing slippers until they glittered like the sparkles from her wand. Then, with a final flick, a heart-shaped form sprinkled with pale golden yellow diamonds appeared on the toe of each foot. "Mustn't forget the heart stones."

Petronela performed the opening steps of one of the walking dances. "Esmerelda, I could dance till midnight in these."

"A gown and shoes made out of mementos from those who love you," said Esmerelda. "They will help give you courage."

BACK IN THE COTTAGE, Esmerelda sank into her chair by the fire and put her feet up. She was content with her work. Especially the dress. It would be one to go down in history.

"You were gone a long time," Nadzia said, pouring them each

a cup of tea. "If you hadn't come in when you did, I would have gone to check on you. Were the animals giving you trouble?" Nadzia handed Esmerelda one of the cups. "This will warm you up."

"Thank you. The animals are fine. I've been thinking about the ball tonight. Wondering how the young ones are getting on."

"Oh, I imagine it's a splendid night. Petronela will be wearing the dress Marek sent her. I can't wait to hear how much he surprised her with it."

"Yes. Lots of surprises on a night like tonight." Esmerelda took a sip of the hot tea and wondered if she'd done enough. She suspected Petronela was in more trouble than any of them knew.

A dress and shoes and a carriage might not add up to much, but that was the role of a fairy godmother. She gave a hand. Provided the tools. After that, it was up to the girl to make the best of the situation.

Nadzia laughed as she settled into the chair across from Esmerelda. "Wish I could see what was happening right now. Do you think anyone will recognize her out of those rags?"

"We can speculate all we like, but we'll have to wait until tomorrow to hear any news. Drink your tea."

as this really happening? Petronela squeezed the leather seat beneath her. The carriage felt real enough. When she tapped her glass shoes against the solid metal, they made a pleasing *ting, ting* sound. And the beautiful white horses racing up the cobblestone road bringing her closer and closer to the castle were certainly real.

If she hadn't seen it with her own eyes, she wouldn't have believed it. Shunned, ignored, outcast Esmerelda was a fairy godmother.

"We are all image bearers of God, Petronela," her mother used to say. "Treat others accordingly." That directive had been tested greatly since her mother had died. How do you treat others who mistreat you? None of that mattered now. The question for tonight was how would Marek and his parents see her?

Her stomach began to twirl as her carriage pulled up to the castle. This was it. Would they remember her? Remember her father? Of course, they would. He and the king had been friends.

Thanks to Esmerelda, she already felt like a princess, albeit one with a worry or two. With peace across the mountain so tenuous, would Marek be able to convince his family there was another way for their kingdoms? As far as what the king and queen thought of her, shedding her work dress went a long way to showing them who she was inside. Would it be enough for them to consider the possibilities?

ALTHOUGH SHE'D VISITED the castle before, she'd never stepped foot onto the black and white checkered marble floor of the ballroom. That had always been reserved for adults.

She didn't know where to look first. Great arches spanned the roof and delightful frescoes of cherubs and angels filled the ceiling. The crystal chandeliers lit the marble room like tiny stars brought down from the sky. Across the room, the thrones were empty, waiting for the arrival of the king and queen.

The line of guests in front of her moved, and she took another step forward. The town crier stood at the top of the stairs announcing guests as they arrived. When Petronela's turn came, she felt a wave of approval coming from him, which boosted her confidence.

Below them, the room was full of guests dressed in their very best and standing at attention, waiting for the dancing to begin. Quickly, Petronela scanned the women and found her stepfamily standing near the punch table. She was beginning to see them more and more as *steps* than as blood relatives. Fortunately, they weren't paying any attention to the arrivals. After all, they, the most important people, were already there. She hoped their inattention continued until after she'd been announced.

"Petronela Bachleda, daughter of General Dominik Bachleda."

Her stepmother looked up, as the name of her husband must have filtered through the noise. Petronela quickly descended the stairs, putting a countess in a large wool hat between them. No sense causing trouble at the start of the evening. She was only here for one thing, to meet and impress Marek's family.

Slipping through the crowd—all these girls—she tried to find Marek. *Where is he?* She felt a heartwarming sensation from her left and turned. *Marek.* Their gazes locked.

He started for her, and as he walked, the crowd between them parted, every gaze following his movements. When he reached her, he held out his hand, a huge smile on his face. "Welcome back to my house."

Nela slipped her hand into his and then followed as he led her to take their place on the dance floor.

"This is the only way we'll get some privacy to talk," he said. "When I'm standing still, they flutter around me like a flock of doves."

She grinned as he put one hand around her waist. "I did notice the crowd was thickest around you."

"Somehow a rumor went out that I was looking for a bride."

Nela maintained her smile, not taking his bait. "They are all very lovely."

"I'm holding lovely," he murmured in her ear.

A royal fanfare interrupted them, and Marek stood at attention. The king and queen entered from a narrow set of stairs to the side of the room. The queen walked in front, dressed in a red wool gown embroidered in gold eagles, her gray hair swept up and secured with a dainty tiara. The king, in matching jacket and traditional wool pants followed.

Nela dipped into a deep curtsy, hearing the rustling of a hundred others doing the same.

Marek touched her elbow and she stood. As they waited for the music to begin, Nela found it hard to concentrate. Strong emotions roiled around her. The young woman beside them emanated jealousy, even as she avoided eye contact. Thick envy rose from the girl behind her, and boredom from the man next to her.

Esmerelda was a clever one. Petronela felt the emotions of people around her merely by being near them.

And Marek! In Marek's presence was a love so strong it almost hurt to breathe. With every touch, her heart raced and any doubts she may have been harboring about him fell away.

The orchestra struck their first chord and the *chodzony*, a walking dance, began.

An elegant partnered dance, they would walk around the ballroom holding hands, with the king and queen presiding. As each couple walked past the thrones, they would be scrutinized by the queen and hopefully obtain approval from the king.

Marek lifted his hand high, and she placed her gloved hand in his.

Petronela tried to tell herself this was no different from practicing the dance with Nadzia in the meadow, but it was. For one, she wore a proper dress instead of her raggedy old frock. For another, people were watching, and that knowledge made her nervous and awkward.

Marek gave her a quick wink before they turned, heads held high, to face the king and queen. "Smile," he said as they began the promenade in time to the music. First, one long step, then two shorter steps.

She tried to hold her gaze up to look at the queen and king, but as they got closer, she dropped her lids in what she hoped looked like a show of respect, not nerves or fear.

After the first walk around the ballroom, the couples split, with women in the center. Nela curtsied, while Marek bowed, and for a moment, as their eyes held, they were the only two in the room. But the music continued and they had to dance with the others. Around the room again, and then before the king and queen, they formed a bridge with their hands while the other dancers ducked underneath.

Petronela reached out for what the king and queen were feeling. Approval and pride from the king. Now, was that for his son, or for his son's choice of dance partner? The queen was mixed. She was feeling mostly love, but also a little bit of sadness.

Petronela glanced up at her, and the queen shifted her attention toward her. Petronela automatically gave a tentative smile and the queen returned it.

At the end of the dance, the king and queen stood and clapped for the dancers while those on the dance floor bowed and curtsied.

Marek pulled Nela up. "There, the ice is broken," he said. "Think you can relax on this next song?"

She lifted her eyebrows questioningly. "Are you saying I was stiff?"

He laughed. "I've seen you more at ease."

There was something else Nela was feeling from the direction of the king, but she couldn't put words to it. Something was not right with him. It wasn't malicious. Maybe worry. Possibly illness? Just when she thought she'd figured it out, someone with strong emotions would get too close, and she'd lose it again. When it was quieter, she'd have to ask Marek if something was amiss at the castle.

The orchestra began again and Petronela focused less on pleasing the king and queen and more on being present for Marek. Soon, she began to enjoy herself and was able to filter out the jealous feelings which floated like a cloud from all the young ladies on the dance floor.

"Thirsty?" Marek asked after they had danced for hours.

"Yes, please." Petronela eyed the long tables filled with crystal bowls of raspberry kompot along with bite-sized biscuits and cakes with shiny white icing.

He excused himself, and then returned with a glass of kompot. "Catch your breath while I dance the zbojnicki with the men. I haven't danced it since my brother died. After that, I'll introduce you to my parents. It looks like my father is almost finished with the dignitaries."

She sipped while watching Marek, full of life and energy circle up with the men for the start of the dance. It was good to see him so burdenless. Her dad had also loved this dance. He said a man had to have strong legs to dance the zbojnicki.

The men began to march around, each with a highlander's walking stick, the *ciupaga*, which had an axe head atop the long handle. As the dance grew more exciting, with axes swinging and men jumping, the people began to clap with the music.

Near the end of the dance, Petronela downed the sweet drink and then looked for a servant who would take her glass. She ought to be ready to meet Marek's family. Ah, there was a man standing to the side of the room, near the great doors leading into the garden.

After she placed her glass on the tray he held, she felt a sharp coolness in the air and spun around, trying to find the source. A darkness pushed against the love and it made her shiver. She looked for Marek, but he was hard to find in the moving crowd.

When she turned around again, her stepmother blocked her way, arms crossed. "You made it after all."

CHAPTER 21

*P*etronela's throat went dry. She knew this moment would happen eventually, but she'd hoped to have Marek by her side when it did. How could this woman intimidate her so? She settled for "I was invited just like every other girl here."

"Yes, but you know what I am trying to do for my daughters. You're getting in the way."

At the tone of Marzena's voice, Nela's blood grew cold. She'd been scared of Marzena before, but this time the feeling went through to her bones. *Her stepmother wouldn't harm her, would she?*

Marzena took a step forward, pushing Nela close to the curtained window.

"What do you want?" Nela asked. She held Marzena's dark gaze, chin held high.

"I'm glad you asked. Walk with me in the garden." She grabbed Petronela's arm and pulled her toward the nearest door.

"I'd rather stay here," she said, freeing herself. "It's almost midnight and Marek will want to dance the *mazur*."

Her stepmother scoffed. "I saw you in the walking dance

when the ball began. You looked ridiculous, strutting around like you believed you belonged." She mimicked a spin. "Your shoulders slouch on the turns. Really, you should practice more."

Nela had enough. Her stepmother could treat her horribly in their home, but they were in Marek's home now. She didn't have to stand here and take it. She tried to push past, but Marzena was quick, catching her arm again in an iron grip.

Before Petronela could pull away, Marzena shoved her out onto the dimly lit patio. Marzena nodded to someone who came up from behind and grabbed her other arm.

"Help!" Petronela called out, but the orchestra drowned out her voice. No one heard her. She spun around trying to see who was helping Marzena, and her heart sank as she recognized him.

The tutor who came from across the mountain grimaced down at her. "Quit struggling." The hatred emanating off him was stronger than that of her stepmother. *Why did he care anything about her?*

They shoved her down the stairs and into the back garden, barely giving her time to get her feet under herself.

"Leave me alone," she said, struggling. "I have a right to be here."

"It's almost midnight. The ball is ending anyway." Marzena kept up the fast pace.

"You're taking me home now?"

On a landing on the stairs, Nela dropped limply to the ground. It was an effective technique she'd seen toddlers in the marketplace use on their mothers.

But the tutor scooped her up, pinning her arms so she couldn't hit him. She kicked and tried to hurt him with everything that was in her, but he was tougher than he looked, absorbing all her efforts.

Finally, her shoe caught in her dress, falling off. The cold air bit at her right foot.

"Wait. My shoe."

They continued their hectic dash down the stairs away from the castle.

"It's freezing, at least get me my shoe." That beautiful glass slipper. What would she tell Esmerelda?

"You'll be a lot colder soon," the tutor said in a low voice.

Petronela's thoughts raced as she was carried away through the juniper bushes. If she could get away from the tutor, she could make a run for it. Take off her other shoe and run. Her feet had toughened up from going without shoes for most of the summer. The dress would make it hard to run, but if she could find a place to hide, she might have a chance.

She passively waited for the tutor to get used to her dead weight. But when she saw Marzena's carriage tucked away, her heart sank. They'd planned this out. They would have had time during the dancing.

She couldn't let them get her into that vehicle. With all her strength she fought off the tutor. Still, he was too strong. She managed to scratch at his face, and jab at his eyes, but he quickly had her subdued.

Petronela had spent plenty of hours angry and frustrated at her situation, but she'd never been this angry and frustrated before. She'd underestimated her stepmother's vindictiveness.

Marzena opened the carriage door, and then the tutor shoved her in. Petronela fell across the back seat and immediately crawled toward other side. The tutor grabbed her bare foot.

"Nela!" Marek's voice cut across the clear night. He was in the garden.

She sat up and scooted back to the open door. "I'm—" a gag was shoved into her mouth. The tutor had a rope in his hand and he worked at tying her hands together.

"Nela, are you out here?"

"Mmm." She tried so hard to escape, but she couldn't. Tears of frustration squeezed out of her eyes.

"Take her. I'll deal with the prince." Marzena smoothed her

skirt and pasted on a fake smile before walking back through the junipers.

CHAPTER 22

In the early hours, Esmerelda lay staring up at the beams of her cottage. She'd been awake all night, too excited and satisfied from her activities to fall asleep. It had been a long time since she'd gone to such great lengths to help a girl with her happily ever after.

Resigned to no sleep, she got up and started the fire to take the chill out of her bones. Based on the drifts along the windowsill, it had snowed all night.

Then she took up her tatting she'd left on the arm of the rocking chair.

Across the room, Nadzia stirred in her small bed. "I wonder how the night went," she said, staring dreamily into the flames.

"It's not quite morning yet," Esmerelda whispered. "Go back to sleep."

"Wish I could have been there. I've never seen a ball, and I know most of the dance steps."

Esmerelda looked up after making a double knot, a shocked look on her face. "You never said you wanted to go."

The fire popped in the background as a log broke in two.

"Forgive me." Esmerelda frowned as she pinched the thread. "I should have known you'd want to go. You're not such a little girl anymore. I would have helped you go, too."

"Even though I'm too young to join the adults in the dancing? Besides, you'd be all alone up here."

Esmerelda's heart squeezed. *I knew taking her in was a bad idea. She's made me soft, and I've made her dependent. I should have tried harder to find her mother. Or a barren woman who would have made a better mother than me.*

"Nadzia, your first thoughts shouldn't be worry for leaving me all alone."

"But—"

An insistent pounding at the door startled them both. *Who would be here so early in the morning?*

When Esmerelda opened it, Marek burst into the room, bringing with him a swirl of snowflakes falling onto the rag rug. "Is she here?"

His eyes were wild, desperate.

"Petronela?" Esmerelda said the name with trepidation.

"She's not at home—none of them are—and I found this." He held up a delicate glass dancing slipper, sparkling with diamonds. "It was on the stairs in the garden."

Nadzia gasped.

"Yes, that's hers," Esmerelda confirmed.

"A woman said she saw Petronela running off with a chap with a mustache and then others said they saw the couple sneaking off together as well."

Esmerelda's mouth formed a tight line.

"She wouldn't," Nadzia said. "You know that, don't you?"

He nodded. "I think they've taken her someplace. Could you do something?" He looked at Esmerelda expectantly.

She cocked her head. "Start at the beginning. Go slowly."

"There's no time. We were dancing. She was beautiful. I thought I'd convinced her that we could be together. Then she was gone. She had said she ought to leave by midnight to get home before her family, but that's when my father was finally finished with the cabinet members. I was going to introduce her after the men's dance, but when I came back for her, she was gone. I went looking for her and caught a glimpse of her gown at the edge of the garden. At first, I thought she'd gotten tired of waiting. Maybe changed her mind. But I went to her home and it was empty. Can't you do something?"

Nadzia shook her head. "She loves you. She has from the day she saw you in the meadow."

But the prince wasn't looking at Nadzia.

Esmerelda narrowed her eyes. "What are you asking me?"

He glanced at Nadzia and back again. "I've heard things about you."

Fairy godmother.

Esmerelda kept her face blank.

"She's in trouble and I can help her, I know I can." Marek reached a hand out in a pleading motion. "She said her stepfamily has connections to the Burgosovs across the mountains. What if they plan to use her to get to me? We have to act fast."

Time to move along.

"I'm an old woman. What can I do?" She shuffled her feet to the table to emphasize her age and try to make him think before asking his next question. *I'll need a place for Nadzia.*

"You can help me find Petronela." He looked wildly around as if searching for answers before he held out the shoe. "Here's a connection to her. Can you use this to lead me to her?"

Esmerelda had expected him to ask her to wave her wand and bring her home, or send him to her. Big requests that would make her interfere more than she was allowed. This lad showed promise. "You're a clever one, aren't you?"

"If by clever you mean desperately in love and in need of your help, then, yes."

"I think I can help you after all." She handed him the water bucket. "The well is near the garden."

He took the bucket. "Are you making a potion?"

"Tea." She crossed her arms. "I need time to think about this one and thinking always goes better with a warm cup."

He hesitated, then opened his mouth, closed it, and shot out the door for the water.

"We have plenty of water already," said Nadzia, putting the kettle on the stove. "Why would he think you would make a potion?"

Esmerelda stood. "He's a doer. He needs to stay busy, and why waste help from a prince when you can get it?"

Nadzia smiled through her sadness. "Can you really help him find her?"

"I can provide him with the means, but the rest is up to him." Esmerelda began to pace. "Go outside and give me a minute. Before you go, hand me that shoe. I have an idea."

Esmerelda cracked open the window while Nadzia met Marek at the well.

"She kicked me out, too. She needs time to think in quiet," Nadzia said. "Why did you come to Esmerelda for help? I mean, she's wise and all, but a problem like this should go to the king, if you don't mind my saying."

"Oh." Marek filled the bucket and set it on the stone ledge. He paced with his hands locked behind his head. "You think Esmerelda is just a mountain woman."

He glanced up and Esmerelda caught his gaze through the window. She slowly shook her head. *I've not told her.*

"Not *just* a mountain woman," Nadzia said. "The mountain people are more worthy than town folk give them credit for."

"Yes. I trust Esmerelda for the best...advice."

"They wouldn't hurt Petronela, would they?" Nadzia asked.

Marek's face hardened. "They won't be kind."

"Children," Esmerelda called out the window. She'd seen enough. Mulled it over enough. She waved her wand, and it was done. "I've got it."

The two returned to the house in haste. If Marek was offended at being called a child, he didn't show it. *Good*. He passed another test.

"How does it work?" Marek said, staring at the shoe Esmerelda held out with two hands.

"Simple. Ask: 'Where is your partner?'" After the words were uttered, a light traversed the shoe from heel to toe.

Nadzia squinted, cocking her head. "What was that?"

Eagerly, Marek took the shoe and tried it himself. The beam of light traveled through the shoe again.

Esmerelda studied Nadzia's reaction carefully. "I made these shoes for Petronela, and now Marek can use them to find her. She's that way." Esmerelda inclined her head in the direction where the toe was pointing.

"Follow the light?" Marek asked.

"And you'll find love," said Esmerelda. It pleased her whenever she could add a bit of style to a wish. "What do you think, Nadzia?" Esmerelda considered showing her wings, but she didn't want to give Nadzia too much of a shock. "Those stories I've told you about fairy godmothers? I have personal experience in that area."

Nadzia was silent as she stared questioningly at Esmerelda.

"It's pointing over the mountains," Marek said, focused on the shoe and not on Nadzia's reaction. "They wouldn't risk crossing over this time of year, would they? Avalanches?"

Esmerelda broke her gaze with Nadzia. "All I can tell you is the other shoe is that way."

He breathed in deep. "Then that's the way I'll go."

CHAPTER 23

*N*adzia made for her coat. She could only focus on one big problem at a time. As if living with a fairy godmother and not knowing it were a big problem. She pushed her questions aside so she could focus on her missing friend. Once they had Petronela back, she would ask Esmerelda to tell her everything.

"If the Burgosovs have Petronela like you think they do, you'll need a plan. They'll recognize you, and you'll never get near her."

"Possibly. We'll worry about that when we figure out what's going on."

Nadzia studied his profile. He was too nonchalant, which made her suspicious. "You can't trade your life for hers," she said. "She wouldn't want that."

His jaw clenched. "I'll do whatever it takes."

"We should look for Janosik, the peddler," Nadzia said, checking her coat for mittens.

"We? No. You stay here."

"He's a friend," she said, ignoring Marek's protestations.

"The infamous Janosik? I've heard things about him, too."

"My friend, Janosik." She slipped her coat on. "Janosik isn't a fairy godfather, is he?" Nadzia could never look at anyone now without wondering about them.

"He is not," Esmerelda said. "Are you sure you're okay, Nadzia? It must be a shock what you've learned about me today."

"I'm fine. I want to help find my friend."

Marek held up his hands in protest. "Nadzia, you should stay here. You're too young and it's too dangerous. I'm even going to leave my horse behind. With the fresh snow the way is too unstable. The snow can shift quickly." He swallowed. "I know."

Nadzia pulled on her hat. "I should go with you. I know what Janosik looks like. Esmerelda? Please. It's for Nela, and Marek will look less like an angry prince if I'm traveling with him."

"But the snow in the mountains," Marek said, also pleading his case. "And she's so young."

Marek and Esmerelda stared at each other trying to decide.

Marek looked like he was about to say no, but then seemed to yield to Esmerelda. "I'll keep her safe," he finally said. He held up his highlander's walking stick.

"Of course, you will," Esmerelda said. "Wrap up and stay warm. Here are some hot barley packs for your pockets." She pulled them out of her own pockets, but Nadzia knew there'd been nothing there before.

Dumbfounded, Nadzia accepted two packs and tucked them into her coat. How could she miss all the signs? Esmerelda's efficiency. Her uncanny ability to pull things out of the pantry at a moment's notice.

"Thank you," Nadzia said. It seemed that as a fairy godmother, Esmerelda would give them the tools they needed, but wouldn't go with them. It felt like this was a test for herself as well, and wondered if Esmerelda would be here when they got back.

Suddenly feeling older, Nadzia quickly strapped her snow shoes to her back. They didn't need them now, but they would in the high pass. If they were quick, they'd cross over by nightfall. Marek had longer legs, and she might slow him down, but then again, she grew up in these mountains and was used to the climb and elevation.

If the snow wasn't too soft, they may even make it as far as the peddler's cottage tonight. Being the first house they'd come to, it was close enough to make in one day. In the summer.

Dawn broke as they stepped outside, turning the sky a pale vanilla. The clear sky indicated the day would be cold, and indeed, their breath came out as frozen crystals as they made fresh tracks in the new snow.

Normally, Nadzia loved the first snowfalls. To her, the mountains were home. Beautiful in each season, they seemed especially decorated when the snow came and covered the trees. But it was hard to enjoy the fresh snow when her legs were racing after Marek and her mind was racing with thoughts of secret fairy godmothers.

As they worked their way up the mountain, she began to regret insisting she come. He could travel much faster without her. After the twentieth time he'd wrinkled his brow looking at the mountain, she had to say something. "You seem extra worried."

"It's the sun. That day—it was like this. Fresh snow and a melting sun."

"We'll be careful."

Marek shook his head. "I've gone over that day a thousand times, and I can't think of what else I could have done differently. It was the largest avalanche this area had ever seen. I was found at the edge, where my brother had shoved me, but they found him farther down the mountain where he'd been swept away."

"I'm sorry. But if there's nothing you could have done differently, why do you keep reliving it?"

"Because I wish I could go back and change things. Maybe if I hadn't called out for Nikodem to help me. But it all happened so fast."

"What was he like?"

Marek laughed. "My brother was a playful bear. Fiercely protective of me, and he wanted to try anything. Do everything."

"I think Petronela is like your brother. Or she used to be when she was younger."

He nodded slowly. "Yes. When we were kids, I remember she'd play all the games, even the ones the other girls sat out. Now she is all about responsibility. She ought to feel like she can have fun again."

"Sounds like you two have that in common."

Their conversation ceased as they focused on climbing an especially steep and slippery section. Nadzia's fingers were cold, but she needed to keep her hands out of her warm pockets for balance. Fortunately, the barley packs Esmerelda had given them were still warm even after hours of walking. Nadzia wondered how long they would radiate warmth—for the day? The trip?

Eventually they came to a flatter portion where the snow was soft and up to their knees. They stopped to strap on their snowshoes.

"And what about you?" Marek asked. "What does your future look like?"

"I'll stay with Esmerelda, of course." *A fairy godmother.*

"Don't you want to move into town?"

"I'm fine in the cottage. There's lots of work with the garden and the animals."

He frowned.

"What is it?" she asked.

"You know her better than I do, but Esmerelda seems restless to me. She fidgets a lot and studies you when you're not looking. Nela thinks you might want to move into town. If her living conditions were better, she would have already invited you, I think."

Marek's words resonated more than she cared to admit. Esmerelda *was* restless. And she kept dropping hints about Nadzia needing more than her solitary mountain life. And now with this latest revelation, it might mean that Esmerelda was wanting a change.

"I don't know her as well as I thought I did. Even you suspected she was a fairy godmoth—"

Suddenly, a rumble began high above them. Nadzia took a moment to process what was happening. "Marek?" she said. She tried to keep her voice calm, but they only had seconds to move. Which direction should they go?

Marek scanned the snow line. Nadzia couldn't see anything yet, but by the time they could, it would be too late.

"Forward!"

He pushed her, and she ran. The snow was like mud trying to slow her down. "I can't make it," she said. "You go. Find Nela and bring her home."

Next thing, her legs were swept out from under her, and she closed her eyes, preparing for the snow to swallow her up. She hoped it wouldn't hurt. So far, it felt like floating and she could still breathe. Maybe she could ride it to the bottom. As long as she didn't hit a tree.

"Almost there."

Marek's voice was so close it was in her ear. Was he keeping up with her as they tumbled down the mountain? She opened her eyes and his face was right there. He was carrying her as he ran. She smiled at him. "Thank you." Then the snow hit.

In her eyes, her ears, her mouth.

She was torn out of Marek's arms.

CHAPTER 24

*S*o cold. Dark.

On all fours, Nadzia struggled to steady her breath.

When she was first swept away, she did all she could to stay afloat above the snow, but it sucked her down. Now she was encased with a very small space left around her head giving her a pocket to breathe in.

Totally disoriented, she couldn't tell which direction was up and which was down. She'd heard that could happen in an avalanche. Until she figured out which way was up, there was no use in trying to dig herself out; she might be digging herself further in.

The best thing she could do for herself was to keep a clear head. She started to say a quick prayer, but then decided to keep on talking to God. No one else knew where she was, and she didn't want to be alone right now. "What do I do?" she whispered. "I'm so scared."

The silence made her ears ring. Soft sounds floated around her, indicating the snow was settling. She supposed quiet was better than rumbling.

Nadzia focused on the pressure around her to try to

determine what felt like gravity pulling her down. *So hard to decide.* "Where am I?" She was in a crouched position, but with snow all around, was she kneeling on the snow, or was she lying on her back? She could even be lying on her side, for all she knew.

She pushed with her left arm but met resistance immediately, like she would if she was kneeling on the ground. The warm barley packs in her pockets began to melt the snow and relieved the pressure weighing in on her hips. If only she could move her arms, she could reach down and use the packs to give her a bigger air pocket before the snow packed in more tightly as it settled. She tried, but her arms held fast. She was stuck in place, completely helpless to move.

"Marek!" Her voice sounded muffled, even to her. If he was buried as much as she was, then that was it. The end. He couldn't get to her, and she couldn't get to him. They might even be side by side and not know it. And by the time Esmerelda grew concerned over their absence, hours, days even, may have passed. A person wouldn't last the night buried alive like this. She would suffocate before freezing to death.

In the dark, she began to recite prayers Esmerelda had taught her. If she were to meet her creator, she ought to prepare.

Suddenly, a smooth stick came shooting through the snow near her shoulder. Her panicked brain raced. *What is that?* It disappeared and then jabbed near her other shoulder. Realization dawned. It was Marek's ciupaga. He was trying to find her by jabbing his walking stick into the snow and hoping to find something solid. Like her head.

That meant she was facing up and he was above her. She turned her face to the side in case he hit her eye next.

"Marek!" she screamed as loud as she could. She tried to dig upward, but as soon as she did, a sharp pain shot down her right arm. The stick moved away from her. "Marek! I'm here."

With her left hand, she frantically tried to move the snow in front of her. Bits of ice collapsed on her face, freezing her cheeks and filling her mouth, but it was so hard-pressed she couldn't move it. Marek would have to find her fast, or she'd faint from lack of oxygen. "Marek!"

"Nadzia? I'm here."

The walking stick came poking back until it jabbed her thigh.

"Got you!" he said.

The *chink* and *swish* of the ice and snow above her were the most beautiful of sounds. As the weight above her became lighter, so did the darkness around her. *Hurry.* Her head swayed, like she was falling, even though she was still in the grip of the snow.

"Nadzia? I'm almost to you. Hang on for me."

She tried to call out, but couldn't get enough air in her lungs. So, she just rested and tried to keep calm.

Finally, the light broke through, and she sucked in a life-saving breath. Some of the pressure in her lungs released, though it burned like gritty fire. She blinked up at Marek. Clumps of snow stuck to his shirt and pants and his cheeks glistened in the fading light.

"I thought…" he started, "I was afraid… I never should have brought you."

"I'm okay," she said, breathing deeply. "You saved me."

He nodded, also breathing heavily. "We need to get you somewhere warm. You hurt anywhere?"

"My arm. Not sure about anything else yet."

She shivered, and Marek gave her his barley packs. "These will help. Mine are as warm as when Esmerelda gave them to me."

Grateful, Nadzia reached out with both hands, but dropped her right arm in pain.

"You are hurt." He bent down to examine her.

"Yes, my right shoulder and my ankle." She used her good

hand to hold the barley packs to her cheeks, letting both her hand and her face warm up.

"I don't see any bleeding. How far are we from Janosik's do you think?"

Nadzia was a little disoriented. They'd slid off the path and would have to climb back up, through unstable snow. The thought struck her like ice to the heart after what she'd just been through.

"Too far for today." She looked warily up the mountain. "By the time we make it back up there, it'll be dark."

"And you'll be frozen." He handed her the ciupaga. "Let's move to the edge of the avalanche zone and then I'll make a snow cave. We can build a fire and continue on in the morning."

Nadzia nodded. Both those things sounded wonderful.

After stabilizing her hurt arm, he got under her good arm to support her while she stumbled along. It was slow going, picking their way over the rough chunks of ice and soft pockets of snow. With each jolt, pain shot through her shoulder and tweaked her ankle. She gritted her teeth and continued on, one uneven step at a time. Esmerelda's barley bags were enough to keep hypothermia at bay, but that didn't mean Nadzia wasn't freezing. Thoughts of a warm fire kept her going.

"We're almost halfway," Marek said.

It felt like they'd been walking for an hour already. Nadzia groaned. "I can't do it."

"Yes, you can. The more you move, the warmer you'll be. Keep going."

A dog barked in the distance, and they both stopped to listen. Another bark. Soon, Bobik shot into view.

Nadzia was never so happy to see a dog in her life.

"Stay," she commanded as the dog started to cross the avalanche zone. The dog hesitated, but then came forward. "Stay," she said again, firmer.

Bobik whimpered, but sat.

"Good boy. We'll come to you."

"Whose dog?" Marek asked.

Nadzia smiled. "Janosik's. He can't be far behind."

"You sure you trust him? We're on their side of the mountain, now."

"With my life."

Marek nodded, and continued to lead them across the dangerous terrain.

Soon, Janosik's red hat emerged from the trees. He raised a hand in greeting. "Ho there, you all right?"

"Will be, as soon as we get across." Nadzia looked despairingly at the distance yet to go. "Stay there. We'll come to you."

While they continued to make their way to safety, Janosik emptied his sleigh of wood and other supplies he'd been gathering. "I heard the slide and wanted to see the damage," he said. "Never dreamed someone would be caught in it."

Bobik had taken to pacing back and forth along the edge of the rough snow. When they drew close enough, he bounded forward and jumped up on Nadzia.

"Easy there," she said, smiling wide. They'd made it. "Good boy. Now off you go."

Bobik bounded ahead of them, clearly happy the wait was over.

"Me too, buddy," she said as Marek and Janosik helped her onto the sleigh. Once she was settled, she let herself feel the full brunt of what she'd just been through and she shook uncontrollably. Then the tears fell.

CHAPTER 25

*W*hen Nadzia woke, she was warm, but stiff. A wool blanket had been tucked around her, and a small fire crackled behind a grate, casting a flickering light against the rough wooden walls. When she realized she lay on a narrow bed in a shepherd's bacowka, she immediately sat up, looking for Marek.

A stool scraped across the floor as Janosik stood. "Easy, now. I've bandaged your arm and shoulder. Nothing broken that I can tell, but you'll be sore for a few days. You must have hit a rock or two on your tumble."

"Thank you." She tentatively touched her sore places. Already a nasty bruise colored her arm. "Where is Marek?"

Bobik trotted over and sat waiting for a pat. She happily obliged.

"Kapusta?" asked Janosik.

Nadzia nodded, and he placed a bowl of stewed cabbage on a small table for her.

"And Marek?" she repeated.

"He's gone ahead." Janosik put on his coat. "I'll get more

firewood." He walked past the stack of firewood piled neatly against the wall near the door.

Nadzia cocked her head. Janosik was trying to avoid something. "Marek left me?"

Janosik paused with his hand on the latch. "Not exactly. We can follow him when you're rested."

She raised an eyebrow.

"Eat first. Then we assess." Janosik returned to the table and nudged the bowl toward her.

While Nadzia ate Janosik's comforting kapusta, he sat with her and kept up a steady one-sided conversation. Nadzia nodded politely, but her mind was elsewhere.

Marek would make good time hiking down the mountain. At the road, he might find a ride into the capital, but so could she. The difference would be the speed she'd be hiking with Janosik. He was unsteady on his feet and couldn't be hurried.

"What do you know about the Burgosovs?" she asked.

He glanced at Bobik. "Stubborn and defensive as a dog with a new bone. They are a wealthy family, looking to take over the kingdom. With no heir on this side of the mountain, all the influential families are vying for position in the kingdom. The Burgosovs have many children so heirs are not a problem for them. I don't know why they would take your friend against her will."

"They might not have, but they are the ones with the most to gain from Petronela's disappearance."

"I admit I saw the Burgosov tutor rush by my house late in the night. My house is north of here, along the main route. This man has crossed the pass often enough in the last few months. If the Burgosovs are involved, the plan is poorly thought out."

Nadzia pushed the bowl away. Her stomach churned with too much worry for her to eat any more. "Petronela said a tutor from across the mountain had been visiting her house. Would he act on his own accord?"

"It's possible." Janosik took her bowl to clean it. He held his hand up when she tried to help.

"We should set out immediately. Otherwise, Marek will sacrifice himself to save Petronela." She heard the panic in her own voice.

Janosik's wizened eyes softened. "Why do you think this is his only option, to trade his life for hers?"

Nadzia was taken aback. She'd just assumed. "It's the fastest way, and he looked determined. He might think it's inevitable because there are so many reasons for him to agree to the marriage. To make everyone else happy by bringing peace."

"Can there be peace that is forced this way?"

"Probably not, at least not in Marek's own household. How could he ever forget how the marriage came to be?"

"I don't know your friends well, but from what I know of Marek, you can trust him to do the right thing." Janosik said. "He was with those who negotiated the peace treaty. He shows wisdom for someone so young."

"All the same, I should be there to help my friends."

"Nadzia, you're injured." His words were gentle as if speaking to a little bird.

"You've known me from a baby. I'm a mountain girl, and I'm strong. You think a little snow will stop me?" She tried not to think about the avalanche, but put her friends first. She would be useful to Marek and Petronela. No one knew who she was or that she was friends with the prince. Like Esmerelda, she could get by on the edges, helping, but unexpected. "Marek is smart, but also in love. He might not be thinking clearly." She frowned thoughtfully. "Though, if it were me, I would pretend to agree to a marriage, and then escape."

Janosik winked. "So would I. And they would expect that."

"We have to go after them, now." She pointed at Janosik. "You have a reputation for being clever, what would you do?"

He laughed, a dry raspy sound of age. "Not with intrigue of

the heart. Perhaps in my youth, but not now. I can get you into the Burgosov place without anyone knowing. After that, it's up to you."

"What do you suggest?"

"I'm friendly with the cook, who is friendly with the lady's maids. It's always wise to keep the women in the castle happy—both the royals and the servants. The men might fight in the wars, but it's the women who make things happen."

Nadzia smiled. "No wonder Esmerelda likes you so." She let her smile fade. "I feel I've led too sheltered a life. I can't understand why this is happening. When I was little, I loved it when the winged warriors galloped by our cottage. It was like a parade marching by just for us. But Esmerelda wouldn't clap and wave with me. Of course, I'd cover my ears when they got close because the pounding hooves and clattering feathers were too much for me. I didn't know what the parade meant until one day, on a returning trip, I suddenly realized the stains on their uniforms were blood and the soldiers lying across the horses weren't sleeping."

Janosik smiled wryly. "We gain new perspective when we grow up. It's not always a better perspective, eh?"

"No." Though she supposed she was glad to know things now. She took a step toward the door. "Shall we go?"

"Right away. The good news with all this snow, is that it's a lot faster to go down the hill than up. You ready for a sleigh ride?" He opened the door and a blast of cold air rolled into the room.

She shivered as the cold overtook the warmth of the fire. Suddenly, it was like she was buried again, trapped under the weight of snow. Quickly, she stood before her fear paralyzed her, and she followed Janosik outside. One step at a time until Petronela was home again. Then there would be time to explore all the emotions.

"I almost forgot." Janosik went back into the hut and came out with something pinched between his fingers. "Marek said it fell out. No clue what he was talking about. Make sense to you?" He placed a small yellow diamond from the heart stone into her palm.

Nadzia's eyes widened. *That Esmerelda is so clever.* "I suspect we'll have an opportunity to use this soon."

CHAPTER 26

*N*adzia shouldn't have doubted Janosik. He was a resourceful man, and by twilight, they were standing in front of the back door to the Burgosov manor house. Descending into town, they had left the snow behind, but it was still cold. With a wave, the man with the pony cart continued on his way, filled with local news from Janosik to spread to other towns.

"Janosik! Welcome in," said the cook with arms wide open. She was a woman with graying hair, who obviously partook of her own cooking. "With the weather, I didn't think I'd see you again until spring." She gave him a hearty hug, despite her dirty apron.

"My visit is unexpected to me, too. This is my friend, Nadzia." Janosik waved her forward.

"Pleased to meet you, my dear." The cook squeezed her arm. "Hungry? I need someone to taste my soup and give me an opinion." The cook led the way into the depths of the kitchen where food was piled up on counters, and pots smelling of beef and rosemary simmered over the hearth fire.

"Smells delicious." Nadzia squeezed past the two girls chopping vegetables.

"Sit right here, miss," the cook said, placing a small wooden chair against the wall and out of the way. She then turned to Janosik. "I'm sorry I cannot sit and talk, old friend." She shoved a basket of beets at him. "Wash these, will you?" She returned to the pots. "Got a big dinner to prepare for tonight. A prince is in town and we need to impress him."

Nadzia glanced at Janosik.

The cook winked at Nadzia. "I'll be cooking for a wedding soon, mark my words." The cook scooped out a bowl of soup and handed it to Nadzia. "What do you think?"

"A wedding, eh?" Janosik casually asked while transferring the clean beets to another bucket. "Who for?"

"The oldest girl, believe it or not. Roksana. Never thought I'd see that happen. She's quiet. Not much to look at, especially with her younger sister standing next to her, but between the two, I don't mind telling you, she's the better catch."

Nadzia bristled at the assessment of the sisters. How terrible to be compared over looks you were born with, as if one could help it. She lowered her eyes and sampled the soup. *Mmm.* "This is wonderful, thank you."

The cook nodded at Nadzia's complement, then continued her conversation with Janosik. "The prince from across the mountain is dining with us for the first time. We've all been told to make a good impression."

Nadzia held her breath and forced herself to not look at Janosik, lest she give away their mission. If Marek was there, that meant the shoe had led him, and that Petronela was nearby.

"If there's to be a wedding, there'll be a need for more lady's maids," Janosik said. "Nadzia here would be of service. She's a handy one. Could help serve at table tonight, if you'd like."

"Oh, I don't need any more for service. You can check with Annushka about maids. She'll be down shortly."

"Annushka is busy, what do you need?" A prim and proper maid stepped in from the hallway. "We don't need any more maids, if that's what you're gaggling after." She looked Nadzia up and down.

"Where in the house do you work?" Janosik asked.

The maid straightened. "Upstairs. I serve Lady Roksana."

Janosik dried his hands and turned his full charm toward the maid. He smiled and gestured to the door. "Let's leave Cook alone while we discuss business."

The maid looked quizzically at Cook, who confirmed his trustworthiness. "If he's offering, I'd be listening."

So the maid went with him to the small courtyard where they grew herbs.

Janosik gestured to Nadzia with pinched fingers. She scrambled for the diamond she'd tucked into her hidden pocket.

"Is there someplace else you might need to go to for a few days? Just to open up an opportunity for Nadzia here to show the family what a good helper she could be."

Nadzia displayed the yellow diamond on her palm where the late afternoon light made it glitter, drawing the maid's attention. She didn't like the idea of putting the maid on the spot like this, but they had to act quickly.

The maid glanced around before answering. "I'm loyal to the family and wouldn't want to see them hurt, despite what you're suggesting there." She licked her lips, eyes fixed on the jewel.

"Nor would we," Janosik said. "You can consult with Cook. I'm as true as they come, and this girl won't cause any trouble. She knows how to keep counsel."

"You'll not be stealing from them?" the maid crossed her arms and stared Janosik down.

He nodded to the diamond. "We've no need to steal."

The conflicted maid scratched under her bonnet. "I do have a sick aunt I've been wanting to see before she passes."

"And so you should," Janosik said. "We never know how long we have on this earth, do we?"

Nadzia quietly held her breath through this exchange. How did Janosik know the maid wouldn't turn them in? He was being very bold.

With one last look around, the girl unpinned her bonnet and shoved it at Nadzia. "You'll have to get through Annushka. I can't help with that. And be kind to m'lady. She's had a bad week."

As the maid scurried off, Janosik whispered, "We've made an opening; now let's try to fill it."

They did not have to wait long for Annushka to appear. Unlike the flurry of the other maids, this woman walked quickly, but with purpose and control.

"Anyone see Lady Roksana's maid?"

Nadzia glanced nervously at Janosik. They'd never be able to fool this woman into believing Nadzia was ready to work as a maid in a proper household such as this. Their plan was too spontaneous.

"Yes," Janosik said, stepping into her path. "She told me to express her sorrow, but that she had to attend to a sickly aunt. Nothing short of heartbreaking disease would have pulled her away from her duties, and also the fact that I had a solution for her, that I hope will also be acceptable to you."

Annushka raised an eyebrow. "And you are?"

"Lifelong friend of Cook's."

Cook waved a wooden spoon in agreement, then went back to stirring.

"All right then." She tilted her head, indicating she'd listen.

"Seems we're both in a bit of a bind," Janosik started out. "I've found myself responsible for this young gal here, but I have no need for her. She's strong and a good worker. Might you have an opportunity here in the house?" He subtly inclined his head toward the bandages on her arms. "She's been through an ordeal."

Annushka *tsked* in sympathy. "And one so young. We work hard in this household, but we're not abused."

Nadzia was about to correct the woman's assumption, but Janosik shook his head slightly.

Annushka scrutinized Nadzia, her gaze lingering on her bandage and frowned. "Do you have references, child?"

"No, ma'am. This would be my first position."

Annushka frowned, and then said, "My maids start in the wash room and earn their advancement."

"Is there any need for her in the house?" Janosik said. "Perhaps serving the one who is about to get married. The girl only needs an opportunity." He subtly inclined his head toward the bandages on her arms, a look of deep concern etched on his face. "The wash room would be too strenuous until she heals."

The cook clapped her hands. "Twenty minutes until first course." She leaned toward Annushka. "I can vouch for them. If Janosik says she's good, she's good."

Annushka flattened her lips into a line before turning her attention to Nadzia. "Mind your manners and be quick to serve." She gave several quick instructions before saying, "Off you go, child. Third door at the top of the stairs. You *can* manage a wardrobe, can't you?"

CHAPTER 27

With heart fluttering, Nadzia pushed open the half-closed door to Roksana's bedroom. The walls were painted white with dainty pastel pink and blue flowers edging the ceiling. Two intricately carved wardrobes, a vanity, and a matching canopied bed filled the space.

The young woman sat in a window seat, a book left unread in her lap while she stared outside.

"Excuse me," Nadzia said. "You've been called to the hall."

The girl turned briefly. "They've given me a new Keeper already?" She made a face. "That was fast."

"Excuse me?"

"Keeper of the wardrobe," she said before gazing back out the window. "Go ahead and pick out a dress for me. Doesn't matter which."

Relieved she was accepted without questions, Nadzia stepped into the room and closed the door.

"One that makes you look your best?" She studied Roksana's dark hair and tan skin tone.

"I said it doesn't matter."

"You don't seem happy about meeting Prince Marek."

The girl turned full around now. She raised an eyebrow. "You're a bold one. And young."

Nadzia curtsied and lowered her head. "I'm new," she explained, keeping her eyes averted. "I'm sorry if I overstepped my place." She hoped her explanation would stand. It wouldn't do to have herself thrown out of the place before she could figure out how to rescue everyone.

"You don't have to cower in front of me. Later, if my parents are in the room, or the general, yes, you must not speak to me so freely. Rise up."

Nadzia obeyed, already liking this girl she was so prepared to...not like. She met the girl's gaze and they both smiled.

"Now, do you think you can choose a dress or will I have to do it myself?" The girl glanced at Nadzia's bandaged arm before turning away.

She must think I was abused, like Annushka assumed. A compassionate adversary. Not what she expected.

After a slight hesitation, Nadzia opened the first wardrobe. She gasped at the most beautiful gowns she'd ever seen. Why ever did someone need this much clothing? Roksana could wear a different gown every day for a month—just in this one wardrobe.

A royal blue silk with a full skirt overshadowed the gowns beside it, and so Nadzia pulled it out. *This would be perfect.*

"Not that one." The girl said, her look unreadable.

"Why not? You would look beautiful wearing it."

Roksana raised her eyebrows. Her look indicated Nadzia had overstepped again.

Servant. Keeper of the Wardrobe. Reluctantly, Nadzia returned the voluminous gown.

The girl sighed as she pushed herself off the window seat. "It's my favorite, and I'll never wear it again."

What an unusual girl. "If it's your favorite..." Nadzia checked herself before continuing. She was supposed to be playing the role of a servant. *Do what I'm told, don't ask questions, and keep my ears open.*

"If you were in love, wouldn't you reserve your favorites to wear only for your love?" said Roksana.

Nadzia was confused. She thought the Burgosov family was clamoring to unite with the royal family across the mountain. Didn't she know Marek would be at the dinner?

"Won't you see your love tonight?" Nadzia asked.

It was the girl's turn to blush.

"So you should wear it, then." Nadzia held out the gown.

Roksana shook her head. "I may never wear that dress again. It'll remain in my wardrobe as a symbol of what I had to give up to keep peace between the kingdoms."

"Your love is not Prince Marek?" *Please be a reasonable person and say it's not.*

"Mother tells me love will grow over time. That I can learn to love him, even if he is a bad man."

Nadzia bit her lip to keep from speaking up for Marek's honor. On this side of the mountain, after surviving the recent conflict, they would have bad feelings towards Marek and his family. But as a servant in *this* kingdom she shouldn't extol the virtues of the prince from over the mountain.

She settled for saying, "He can't be that bad if your parents want you to marry him."

Roksana shrugged. "I wasn't supposed to be important. It's my twin brothers that are in line for the throne, quite distantly I may add. I thought I could talk my parents into letting me marry someone I wanted. My brothers aren't very happy with this latest development either. They wanted to overthrow the kingdom across the mountain, but they can't exactly do that if I'm over there. They'll have to share the power in the region. With me. I don't know, but my brothers will probably overthrow the kingdom anyway." She raised her hands. "Look at me. Talking about power as if I care."

"Sounds like you need to start caring," Nadzia said. *Especially with all this talk of overthrowing.*

Now the girl looked annoyed. Nadzia had pushed her boundaries too far, so she quickly picked out a plain rose-colored dress, well, as plain as a gown like this could be, and shoved it at the girl. "Anything else I can help you with?"

"My shoes. You've never done this before, have you?"

"No, miss."

"What happened to my regular Keeper? I thought I'd treated her well." She frowned.

"Didn't someone tell you? Her aunt is desperately ill, so she's gone to pay her respects. She'll be back soon. I'm sure I can manage to serve you until then."

"Oh, that's sad about her aunt. She obviously didn't ask Mother, who wouldn't have allowed any servant to leave this week. We better keep it our secret. I'll cover for her, but please act more like a trained servant when we're in public." She lifted an eyebrow. "For both our sakes."

Nadzia silently responded with a deep curtsy.

"I'm glad it's possible for you to hold your tongue. I was beginning to wonder."

In no time at all, Nadzia had Roksana suitably dressed and properly coiffed. She stood back to admire her handiwork. "I'm not bad at this," she said.

Roksana laughed. "If only all my problems were as easy to solve as deciding my wardrobe."

Trusting her instincts, Nadzia decided to be as bold as Janosik. "I might know a way we can help each other."

CHAPTER 28

"You sure I won't get caught?" Nadzia followed discreetly behind Roksana. The marble hallway to the dining hall shined in the candlelight in stark contrast to her cozy cottage. She'd never been in such a place of finery. Her stomach fluttered with nerves.

"My mother doesn't know all the servants anyway. She won't know you're new." She casually waved her hand. "Try to blend in. Stand at the wall, and if I make eye contact it means I want you to come to me."

They stepped into the grand dining hall and Nadzia gasped. She couldn't help it. Candlelight glittered from ceiling to floor, illuminating a large table laden with silverware and crystal. Dignitaries arrayed in fine dress stood for Roksana.

If Nadzia were to be Roksana's proper keeper of the wardrobe, she would have to chide her later for letting her walk into this dinner under-dressed. Even if Nadzia's job was short-lived, she wanted to be the best keeper of the wardrobe she could be. The rose gown was fancier than anything Nadzia had seen in her mountain town, but here among dignitaries arrayed in lace and silk, it was quite plain after all.

Roksana gave her a look and then jutted her chin to indicate the wall she should be standing at. Nadzia gave a startled bow and went to take her place near a frowning manservant.

Pulling in a deep, relaxing breath, she surveyed the room. There was the lord of the house at the head of the table. His wife, a stern-faced woman to his right. Two solid young men, similar in appearance and therefore Roksana's twin brothers, sat down from her, and beside Roksana was her sister, already fussing about something.

So, this was the family what was wreaking so much havoc on the small kingdom across the mountain. They didn't seem intimidating seated around the dinner table.

Roksana made her way to the only empty chair at the table, dipping her head and lowering her gaze at the young man holding the back of the chair for her.

Nadzia sucked in a breath. *Marek.*

He seated Roksana, and then looked directly at Nadzia. He nodded ever so slightly before following the lord's lead and sitting again.

Nadzia's stomach knotted tighter. She thought she'd relax once she'd reconnected with Marek, but being in the room with all these high-powered people, well, the reality of the situation hit her hard. Despite the pleasantries, tension filled the room. Indecipherable looks passed over Marek's head, and Nadzia wondered if they had been expecting him to show up to rescue Petronela or if his presence had been a complete surprise.

She couldn't tell if the Burgosov family knew what their tutor had done. They all wore polite smiles like they were out shopping in the market on a sunny day. All except a man with a bushy mustache, who could be the tutor Petronela spoke of. He watched Marek with a smug look on his face.

Maybe Janosik was right. She should have trusted Marek to figure it out. He knew about diplomacy. Her own belief was that everyone should simply behave well on their own. Clearly, that wasn't how the world worked. She stared at the tutor until he felt her gaze and looked at her. She felt her face burn and turned her focus back to Roksana.

As if an invisible cue was given, servants entered the room carrying trays of roast pheasant, jellied meat, stuffed cabbage rolls, and other delicious delicacies. The warm smells filled the air and made Nadzia's mouth water. She tried to blend into the wall, but as the dinner went on, she took a step closer, enticed by the wonder set in front of her.

A server strode by and whispered pointedly, "We could use some help."

"Unless you've got need of changing into a gown, I'm not who you want. I'm but a keeper of the wardrobe." Nadzia was glad of the title and pleased with how easily it rolled off her lips.

The server rolled her eyes and continued on, mumbling something under her breath, and Nadzia stepped back to her place against the wall.

During the meal, the conversation centered around weather and crops. But as bellies filled, tongues loosened and the conversation took a turn.

"So, Prince Marek, is your father tired of war yet? Tired of taking a beating?"

Marek turned to the noble who had spoken, a generously-sized man with a grin on his face, and said, "Why talk of war when we are at peace? Look here, I dine at the lord's table for the first time."

"Have your people recovered, yet?" asked an earnest woman. "I heard the towns were devastated, with so many of the women and children in poverty."

From the tone, Nadzia couldn't tell if the woman was concerned for women and children, or merely interested in the drama of it all.

"If you'd excuse me, Father," Roksana interrupted. "May I go for a walk in the garden? Mother?" Roksana tilted her head in Marek's direction.

Her mother stood, reached out and pulled Marek and Roksana together. "You must see the garden," she said to him. "Imported plants from the four corners of the world."

The lord of the manor stared with a critical look at Marek. Nadzia wondered who was in favor of the alliance between the families. No one seemed particularly joyful at the prospect, except maybe Roksana's mother.

Roksana waved for Nadzia to follow them, and she gladly obeyed. After donning their outdoor gear, the three exited the main house.

"Quickly," Roksana said, putting on leather gloves. She tapped daintily down the stone steps lit by torches.

Marek raised his eyebrows at Nadzia, but followed as a potential suitor would.

Surmising her role as a chaperone, Nadzia kept a few yards back to give the couple privacy, but not too much privacy. At least until they got out of sight of the windows where they could still be seen.

"Servant girl—I'm sorry, you never told me your name—it's safe here," Roksana said. "You may join us."

Nadzia hurried forward under the perplexed gaze of the prince. "You know each other?" he asked.

"Only just," Nadzia said. "She's on our side."

Roksana made an impish face then smiled. "Ready to find your friend?"

"Yes?" Marek said tentatively as he glanced between the two. "Which friend is this?"

"I'm not entirely certain where they would keep her, even if she were here," Roksana continued.

Understanding spread across Marek's face. He quickened his pace and reached into a deep inside pocket of his coat.

"So, tell me what you like best about the garden." Nadzia

pulled Roksana's attention away from Marek. But the garden was dark, lit by only a handful of torches, and the flash from the shoe could not be hidden.

"What's he got there?" Roksana asked, trying to look around to see Marek.

"I don't see anything." Nadzia hedged. Even if Roksana had shown herself to be an ally, if she caught a glimpse of that shoe, all that could change. Jealousy can cause people to do things they never thought they would. For Roksana's protection as well as Petronela's, Nadzia had to do everything she could to keep the shoe a secret.

"What's down here?" Marek asked, pointing to a stone building hidden in shadows.

"The old toolshed. No one uses it anymore."

Nadzia raised her eyebrows and Marek nodded.

"Let's check." Nadzia pivoted to go in that direction.

"Who is she exactly?" the girl asked. "You're taking a big risk for her, especially if she's not here. My brothers are proud and won't stand for a false accusation."

"She's my friend," Nadzia answered. "The first one I ever had. She's done nothing wrong and shouldn't be kept here against her will."

Roksana glanced back at the main house, her loyalties being tested. "If so, there'll be a guard. I can distract him, but that's all."

"Thank you," Marek said. He gave her a genuine smile. "You are not what I thought. My fate would not have been as terrible as I imagined it would be. I wish you well."

Roksana guffawed. "Unfortunately, my sister has a reputation that sticks to me as well." She turned thoughtful as she examined Marek. "I can say the same for you. You're not the warmonger that I expected. I wish you well in your quest for peace. I hope it *is* peace and not conquest. For if it is conquest, my people will be relentless in their response, and I will help them."

"Speaking   officially,   I'm   content   with   my   kingdom's boundaries. I only wish that were true on this side of the mountain."

Roksana was about to answer when they were met by two guards.

"What are you doing out here?" one said, addressing Roksana in a familiar way. A guard she obviously knew. He then cleared his throat and spoke more formally. "This area is restricted."

"I've come to see my new lady-in-waiting. Mama told me she was being kept out here until she received her training. Something about her needing to learn the ways of our household. I'd like to talk to her before Madam Olena gets her fingernails into her."

"We can't do that, miss," said the other guard.

Roksana glanced at Nadzia. Her bluff confirmed Petronela was there.

Marek elbowed Nadzia and motioned that he was going to sneak around them and try to find Nela. "Stay here to help Roksana," he whispered. "I'm not sure how long she can keep them talking."

Nadzia figured the one guard would stay as long as Roksana was here, but the other seemed more intent on his job. He kept his eye on Marek, who was innocently exploring the garden, examining bush and tree as he wandered away from the group.

"I'm new to service," blurted Nadzia. "Do you like working here?"

The guard briefly looked her way before returning his attention to Marek. "It's fine as any other job I've had."

"Where else have you worked?"

"In the army."

"Oh." She wasn't good at this. Marek was now on the periphery and the attentive guard stepped away from the group to follow him.

Nadzia began coughing, like she was near choking.

"Are you all right?" Roksana asked.

"Wa...ter" She waved her hand in front of her throat while trying to signal Roksana she needed her help in distracting the second guard.

Roksana turned to him. "Don't just stand there. Go up to the house and fetch her a glass of water."

"But, Miss..." he looked awkwardly around the garden.

"We're not going to be attacked by the shrubs, but my new Keeper might faint and then you'll have to carry her back."

With a wary glance in Marek's direction, the guard trotted off to the house.

"Let's find a place for her to sit a moment," Roksana said. "The gazebo?"

Nadzia coughed again and nodded meekly. The gazebo was on the far edge of the garden, allowing Marek time to sneak off to the toolshed.

"You stay here, Keeper, while I check on my favorite spruce tree." Roksana wrinkled her brow. "It wasn't looking healthy yesterday, and I wouldn't want to lose it." She turned to her guard and smiled sweetly. "Give me your opinion?"

The guard's gaze fixed on her, he led the way away from the gazebo.

Nadzia didn't wait, doubtful the guard would even notice her if she screamed in his right ear. She hurried to the place where she'd seen Marek step into the shadows. He'd doused the closest torch, so it was especially dark in the shadows of the nearby trees.

As she crept toward the shed, Marek stepped around the corner carrying a rock. He held it up. "To break the lock," he whispered. "How far away are they? Will they hear?"

"Likely, but the guard with Roksana won't think a thing of it. Hurry before the other comes back. He isn't as smitten."

Marek nodded and with a swift *whack*, he hit the lock.

Nadzia pressed farther into the shadows, holding her breath.

They'd have to trust Roksana to keep the guards from investigating.

"You sure Nela is in there?"

Marek nodded before whacking the lock again. This time the door splintered near the handle, and he pulled at the weak place. The door swung open and Petronela burst out and into Marek's arms.

The two embraced, wasting precious seconds.

"I found your shoe," Marek said.

Nela laughed. "You found more than my shoe."

Nadzia tapped Marek's shoulder. "Quickly now. There'll be time for reunions when we're safe." She waved at Nela and ran into the forest.

Janosik said they'd find an old road bordering the property where they could meet him after they rescued Petronela. There was no time to waste.

CHAPTER 29

That brief glimpse inside the toolshed with its stench told Nadzia all she needed to know about how well Petronela had been treated. Nothing good would come of getting caught on this side of the mountain. The sound Marek made pounding at the lock was sure to have brought someone to investigate, no matter how capable at distraction Roksana was.

Nadzia's heart beat fast, prodding her to run through the forest, but Petronela wasn't exactly dressed for the cold or for sprinting. She still wore her gown from the ball, and even with two glass slippers, she was not properly outfitted for sprinting through frosty woods late at night. Marek had to be just as cold as he'd given up his jacket to cover Petronela's shoulders.

They had been slowly and quietly picking their way through the underbrush alongside the dirt road for a long time when Marek voiced her fears. "You sure he said to meet here? Maybe we should circle back. We may have gone too far."

"*Sh.*" Nadzia held up her hand. She cocked her head, straining her ears. *Ca-caw.* The bird call came from their left. "Janosik tried to teach me that same call, but I never did master it like him. This way."

Moments later, they found a two-mule cart, with Janosik in the driver's seat.

"You found the girl." Janosik opened his arms wide in greeting.

"I never doubted we would," said Marek.

"This cart is only available tonight; I'll need to return it soon after dropping you off. It's not the fastest way to travel, but we've got a lead on them. Hop in."

On the journey, Petronela told them what had happened at the ball, how her stepmother, working with the tutor, had kidnapped her and brought her to the Burgosov's house early in the morning. At first, the Burgosovs were perplexed. They didn't understand the gift the tutor was trying to give them. But after the tutor mapped out his plan to unite the kingdoms, they agreed to consider it, banishing Petronela to the shed, away from all the guests they had planned for that night.

"I like to think they would have let me go after a few hours, but as the day stretched, it was as if they'd forgotten about me. I suppose that's when you showed up and priorities changed." She bumped shoulders with Marek. "Had they started bargaining for my life yet?"

Marek shook his head. "I assumed they were waiting until after dessert. They were too busy enjoying jabbing me about the war. After tonight I know that the conflict between our kingdoms is not over."

"And leaving with me will only make it worse."

He rubbed the stubble on his chin. "Possibly. Probably. But there has to be a better way to secure peace in our region."

Nadzia's toes had turned to ice by the time they made it back to the bacowka. She was sure they were being followed, though no one attempted to overtake them. Janosik was aware as well. He didn't glance back as often as she did, but the worry lines on his forehead spoke volumes.

"Someone's there." Marek held up his hand to stop everyone. He pointed to the smoke wisping out of the chimney. "Wai—"

Before Marek could finish his instructions, the door flew open and Esmerelda, cheeks rosy with warmth, welcomed them in.

"I was hoping you all would show up tonight. Got a feast ready for you."

Nadzia jumped down first. "The avalanche. It was dangerous for you to cross it."

"Marek's dog found his way up to my cottage and was concerned, so I thought we'd start walking together and see what we could. I'm glad to find you here and not underneath the snow."

As on cue, the sheepdog burst out the door, tail wagging as he ran toward Marek.

"I was trapped until Marek rescued me," Nadzia said, and Esmerelda's expression flickered concern. "And then Janosik found the two of us."

"And you all found our Petronela."

Nela hopped down next, and soon they had all gathered inside, boots off and toes warm.

"Is the way passable?" Marek asked, looking in the direction of the pass like he wanted to leave that moment. He, too, might have noticed they'd been followed.

Esmerelda glanced at Nadzia before answering. "We shouldn't risk it. Best wait until the area is more stable. A day or two at least."

"That might be too late. We've been followed," Marek said. "I'd prefer getting you ladies back to our kingdom."

"We could end the threat, right now, if you'd like," Janosik said.

"A skirmish on this side of the mountain would be seen as breaking the peace treaty," Marek said. "Maybe that's what they were hoping for—an excuse to start up the fighting again."

Esmerelda spoke up. "Your army is standing by on the other side of the avalanche, waiting for word from you."

Marek gave a wry smile. "Before I left, I told my general to be ready for anything."

Janosik winked at Nadzia. "Violence was not what I meant. There is another way."

To be so jovial at such a time as this. What could Janosik possibly suggest to save them?

"You might be surprised to learn I'm an ordained minister. I can marry you now and neutralize any ideas of joining the kingdoms through marriage. If everyone can stay awake a little longer."

Marek and Petronela looked at each other, love in their eyes.

Good, kind, old Janosik. He didn't want the kingdoms at war either.

"You know we'll have to do this again, publicly?" Marek said to Petronela.

She grinned at him and without hesitation agreed. "Yes, but this time is for us. The second time will be for the kingdom."

Nadzia leaned over and whispered to Esmerelda. "Did you know about Janosik?"

"I'm not surprised. He is a wonder."

"So are you." Nadzia looked pointedly at her before whispering again. "What about a wedding dress for Petronela?"

"Her ball gown is beautiful as is."

"But it's dirty. She's been wearing it for days. A bride ought to have something special, or at least spotless for her wedding, shouldn't she?"

"I might could do something, but how would we explain a wedding dress appearing in the mountains? It's not like we can walk to a dress shop."

"Janosik is the only one who doesn't know. How much do you trust him?"

Esmerelda studied Janosik as he counseled the couple. "Come with me, Nadzia," she said. "We need pure snow."

Thrilled, Nadzia bundled up and slipped out into the dark night with Esmerelda. Before closing the door, Esmerelda said, "When you're done here, Petronela, meet us outside, and we'll adorn you properly."

"What do you two have planned?" Petronela's eyes shone.

"We won't be long," Janosik said. "But if you're going outside, take Bobik with you. He'll let you know if anyone is wandering too close."

Nadzia was glad for the company of the dog, yet she remained alert for any intruders as she followed Esmerelda around the side of the hut. She picked her way past snow dotted with fallen pine needles and other bits of forest detritus to a patch of pure white snow that glittered in the moonlight.

"Can I help?"

"Please. I'll need some things for embellishment. Find something I can use for flowers on the dress and something long for a big beautiful bow at the back. I won't deny I've been thinking about what kind of dress I would make."

Nadzia gathered several pine cones and a nice handful of moss, but when she returned, she found Esmerelda holding a rose-colored ribbon and staring at the snow.

"What's wrong?"

"Oh, nothing." Esmerelda tapped her finger to her lips. "It's just that snow is temporary. The dress won't be as long-lasting as I'd like an heirloom to be."

"Will it last through the ceremony?" She imagined Petronela's dress dripping on the floor as it melted.

"Without a doubt. It'll last for years and years if properly cared for." Esmerelda smiled, like she'd made up her mind. "But I do like the symbolism. A marriage can be a fragile thing. A couple has to work to keep it pure and long-lasting."

"Then what are you waiting for?" Nadzia held out the

embellishments she'd collected. "We've got to hurry before the Burgosovs show up."

"Ah, here she is."

Petronela arrived as Esmerelda took out her wand and, like a conductor, directed the snow to swirl up in the air and envelope the bride in a glittery cloud of ice crystals.

In a moment, the pine cones and moss Nadzia held were pulled into the bright magic that illuminated the forest. In exchange, the ball gown landed in Nadzia's arms. Surprised, she lifted the dress to keep it out of the snow. How did Esmerelda work her fairy magic like this? It was wondrous and familiar all at the same time, and Nadzia wondered if Esmerelda had ever entertained her with magic when she was a fussy baby.

Finally, the glittery whirlwind settled, revealing Petronela wearing a white dress with encrusted diamonds on the bodice. A dusty rose sash positioned at the waist, tied in the back and adorned with large pink rosettes with olive green leaves cascading down the train. The magic light dimmed and they were back in the dark forest.

"Just like I imagined." Esmerelda said with a contented smile before she looked down at the boots peeking out from under the dress. "Make sure to change your shoes when you go inside."

THE CEREMONY WAS A SIMPLE ONE. There were no flowers and very few guests. But there was love and plenty of it.

Nadzia didn't know what the bride and groom thought, but she found the ceremony the most beautiful she'd ever seen, even if it was the only wedding ceremony she'd ever seen. From the way the bride and groom looked at each other, they probably thought they were the only ones in the room.

"The shoes looked whole," Nadzia whispered to Esmerelda. "I couldn't tell where the diamond fell out of the heart stone."

"The diamonds grow back. New diamonds where the holes used to be."

Nadzia was stunned. The more she learned about what Esmerelda could do, the more she was amazed. A seemingly unending supply of diamonds? That fact alone could start a war. Marek was uneasy about the peace. If the Burgosovs found out about the shoes, there would be no peace.

"What can't you do?"

Esmerelda laughed quietly. "Plenty. But I do have fun with what I've got."

Moments after the ceremony ended, the door burst open in a *whoosh* of wind and fresh snow. Two men strode inside, who Nadzia recognized as Roksana's brothers.

"You're too late." Janosik pushed them back into the doorway. "They've already married."

They shoved their way inside anyway. The tall one took a sweeping look over the room, and his eyes lingered on Petronela's shoes. She'd set them near the fire, and they glittered like sunset on a pond.

The heart stones.

He couldn't know about them. Marek had been careful. The guards hadn't seen the shoes and neither had Roksana. Or had she?

Marek stood and took on a protective stance in front of Petronela. "Honor the peace treaty and go home. No more will be said about these last few days. You deal with your people involved in this failed scheme how you see fit, and I'll deal with mine."

While Marek held their attention, Nadzia took a protective stance in front of the shoes.

After a moment of silently staring one another down, the Burgosov brothers moved toward the door. But not without an elbow jab and a jerk of the chin toward the glass slippers. Nadzia crossed her arms and gave the brothers a firm glare.

Janosik closed the door with force and leaned his back against it.

"Well, that's been put off for another day, then," Marek said.

Janosik grunted. "I'll make sure they're going to town. I need to return the cart anyway. Bobik, stay here." He put his boots back on, and Marek joined him.

"Don't worry. They didn't want me to marry their sister anyway," Marek said to Petronela. "They're probably glad things have turned out the way they have. Now they can plot about something else."

Did neither of them notice that the brothers were too interested in Petronela's shoes?

As soon as Janosik and Marek left, Esmerelda let out a deep breath. "Never thought they'd all leave," she said. "Come here, girls." She reached out a hand to each. "Let's make a circle of promise together."

"Did you see?" Nadzia asked. "I think they know something about the shoes."

Petronela glanced at her sparkling dancing slippers. She hadn't known how special they were until Marek explained how he found her and how Nadzia had bribed the maid. "But how could they know?"

Esmerelda shrugged. "Where there's a fairy godmother around, rumors abound. This is why you will need to help each other." She squeezed Nadzia's hand. "Nadzia was left on my doorstep with no family to speak of. Petronela, you have lost your family. I want you to help each other, always."

Esmerelda handed Nela her shoes. To Nadzia she gave the sun-shaped amber necklace from around her neck. "These items work together, and should stay together."

Petronela nodded. "Of course. Nadzia will come with me to the castle, won't you? I'll need your help. You were such a good Keeper to Roksana; you could help me with my wardrobe and so much more."

"The castle? Me?" Nadzia turned to Esmerelda, her mother. "You won't mind, too much? It's not that far away." The look that passed between Esmerelda and Petronela made her wonder if they had been planning this move for a while.

"No, it's not too far away at all," Esmerelda said.

IN THE MORNING, the men hadn't returned yet when there was a knock at the door followed by a friendly hello.

Nadzia opened it to find several mountain folk standing outside with gifts of food. "We heard there was a wedding," said a bright-eyed woman bundled in furs. She carried a dish covered with a towel, steam rising in the cold.

"Come in," Nadzia said, making room. "Did Janosik send you?"

"Only a few of us live up this way, but when we heard you was in need, we got to cookin'."

Another behind her carried what looked like woolen clothes, and she went right to Petronela who was still wearing her wedding gown.

Soon after, the men returned, and they all sat down to warm up and share stories near the fire.

"I hope your love story hasn't spoiled me," Nadzia whispered to Petronela. "My own love affair couldn't be as sweet." She gazed wistfully at the scene before her. A warm fire, a generously shared meal from Janosik's friends, and a grinning bridegroom stealing glances at his new wife.

Petronela smiled knowingly and leaned into Nadzia's shoulder. "It will be sweeter because it will be your own."

CHAPTER 30

"Nadzia!" Nela, now the queen, called for help in preparation for the anniversary ball. "Can you fasten this dress? I think my stomach grew again overnight."

Nadzia laughed. "I'm sure it did. That little one is eager to meet this world, m'lady." She deftly fastened the buttons on the queen's traditional gown. A white blouse with a black bodice over top, embroidered with bright red poppies from Nadzia's own hand, plus a billowy skirt that would match Marek's *parzenica* hearts motif on the front of his cream-colored wool pants. They would make a handsome couple tonight.

Nela pointed to her vanity where a pile of coral wooden beads lay. "I may be a little tense. I broke my necklace. Can't seem to focus on anything right now."

Nadzia frowned. She should have noticed if the threads were loose. "That will take me some time to fix." As keeper of the queen's wardrobe, Nadzia made sure Nela's clothing and shoes and hats and other accessories were maintained in top shape.

"No need. I can go without." Petronela began to pace, wringing her hands.

This time at the ball, there should be no drama, no hysterics, only joy in celebrating Marek and Nela's one-year anniversary. Nadzia said as much.

The queen took Nadzia's hands and waltzed around the room with her. "Next year you'll be of age to join the dancing."

"Even as a servant?"

"You won't be serving, you'll be dancing. You're so much more to me than a servant, you know that, don't you?" Petronela clasped Nadzia's cheeks in her hands. "You've always been a dear friend."

"And as your dear friend, I need you to finish getting ready or your husband will call us out for talking too much."

"I'm as ready as I'll ever be for tonight. Marek will be late, as he and his generals are in a meeting. He sure wishes his father was still here to help him make decisions."

"Sounds serious."

"Nothing too serious to prevent us from a night of fun, yes? I better go down to greet everyone."

Nadzia watched Petronela from the top of the staircase. In the short year Petronela and Marek had been married, the king had died and his wife had become so frail she had taken to her quarters. If it weren't for the promise of a new baby, Marek's mother may have already given up on life.

Important people from around the kingdom would be at the ball tonight, as well as an emissary from across the mountain where relations, though still not friendly, were not openly hostile.

But as Petronela descended the stairs, guards below scattered from their posts, concerned looks on their faces as they raced to other parts of the castle.

"What's going on?" Nadzia asked, hurrying down the stairs herself.

The queen clucked her tongue. "Marek assures me it's nothing to be worried about tonight. I'm sure they are only taking extra precautions. They've had a spy return, but he's in no condition to talk, apparently. They're going to get him some food and rest and see if he'll make any sense."

"By the lines on your forehead you *are* worried." *Not to mention the pacing and the hand wringing and the destroying of beaded necklaces.*

"A spy, Nadzia. I thought we were past all this. I know Marek doesn't want me worrying because of the baby, but..."

"He's right. Enjoy your night of celebration. Soon you'll be too tired for much of anything other than rocking a baby to sleep."

She only said the words to keep Petronela from worry, but while the queen attended the ball, Nadzia planned to find out what was going on from the other servants.

Even though they were now alone in the room, the queen lowered her voice. "If only I could wear the dress tonight. I would have a better idea what everyone was thinking. You don't suppose Esmerelda could fix me another, one that fits me better?" She looked down at her rounded middle.

Nadzia touched her amber necklace, a twinge of guilt reminding her she'd not seen Esmerelda in ages. She hoped her mother didn't think she'd forgotten her now that she lived in the castle. "Esmerelda uses her gifts sparingly, so I think we're on our own."

"Of course. She's already done so much for me."

Nadzia slipped the necklace off and put it around Nela's neck. "Just in case there's something else in this necklace that we don't know about." Esmerelda was nothing if not unpredictable.

"You don't mind?" Nela grasped the amber as if it might provide all the answers.

"You're the only one I'd share it with." Nadzia was an abandoned mountain girl living in the castle—all because of Esmerelda and the queen. How could she not be as generous as they had been with her? And besides, the tension in the house was not related to the excitement of a ball. There was something else rippling through everyone's emotions. Petronela would need all the help Nadzia could give her tonight.

THE BALLROOM DAZZLED with deep-red roses and daisies and lilies brought in especially for the occasion. The large bouquets provided bright splashes of joy against the strained looks and general unease of the servants. The guests were either unaware or too awed by the castle to care if anything was amiss. With beautiful stringed music lightening the mood, how could anything go wrong?

An early snow was falling and guests shook off snowflakes when they stepped inside. *Good. If there was trouble coming from across the mountain, this snow should keep them away until spring.*

Nadzia tried to imagine this same ball a year ago, when Petronela's stepfamily was here, whispering in the alcoves, plotting against her. By the time Marek's men got to the house to arrest them for their part in the kidnapping, they had already left, never to be heard from again.

Nadzia watched from the balcony the whole night, trying to do Nela's worrying for her. Watching especially for any uninvited guests. She didn't trust that the stepfamily wouldn't attempt something on this anniversary night.

A young military man she'd recognized from speaking to Marek walked past, and Nadzia held out a hand to stop him. "Any more news I can tell the queen?" she asked. She hoped he'd assume she knew the basic news and would divulge more than he ought.

"No time to talk." He shook off her hand and continued with purpose.

She'd repeated this with several other servants, and no one knew anything, or they didn't have time to talk. And so, by the end of the evening, with no new disturbances, Nadzia found herself relaxing and watching the dancers instead of the guards. During the traditional dances, she traced steps in the carpet so that she could practice. Perhaps there was nothing to worry about after all. At least, no threat a keeper of the wardrobe could fix.

CHAPTER 31

The next morning, Nadzia tucked the cleaning rag into her apron in exchange for her feather duster. She held it out like a dance partner and placed her other hand against her chest in mock modesty. "You'd like *me* to take this dance?" She looked around as if another maid had entered and was waiting to waltz in her place. "Yes, of course," she said.

Humming the tune from the final song at the anniversary ball, she waltzed on bare toes around the queen's dayroom with her feather companion. She stopped by the door to the queen's bedchamber and pressed her ear to the ancient oak. Not a sound. Should she wake her? Petronela had never slept so late.

No. Let her sleep. Soon there would be no sleep in the household for months.

Nadzia moved on to dusting the vases on the mantel. The round-bottomed red one was her favorite and she took it down to gently sweep the feathers into its neck. It would look lovely with a bouquet of gerberas from downstairs.

"Nadzia!" Petronela's voice carried through the walls.

She ran to the door and flung it open, the vase still in hand. "Yes, my queen?"

Petronela stood by her enormous fireplace, her bedclothes draped gracefully about her large and growing midsection. Her eyes rimmed with red. The door connecting her chambers to the king's shut with a loud *crack*, and she blinked before taking a step forward. Her hands shook as she pulled back her hair and smiled.

"What's happened?"

"You are my most trusted servant and friend. I am sorry to have to send you away."

"Send me away?" Nadzia squeaked. Her breath caught in her throat. To be sent away was to be shamed. What would her mother think to have her stumbling back up the mountain in disgrace?

As if sensing Nadzia's thoughts, Petronela shook her head. Her eyes were kind. "It is because you are my most trusted friend that I give you this task," she said gently. "You will remain in my service, and I will continue to provide for you. You and Esmerelda. You must go to her."

Nadzia's knees regained some strength. The queen was not dismissing her.

"My stepsisters..." The queen's voice faltered. "They have married the Burgosov twins."

Nadzia dropped the vase. Glass shattered at her feet, red shards strewn on the cream tiles like blood.

The queen flinched. "Once they have convinced their husbands to break the peace treaty, they will come for me." She held up a muslin-wrapped package. "They will come for the dress."

Nadzia ran forward, cutting her toe on a piece of glass. She wrapped her arms around Petronela's neck. "Come with me. We will all be safe in the mountains."

Petronela pulled away and pressed Nadzia's hand to her swollen belly. "My time is too soon. No, I cannot make it."

Nadzia felt the skin under the thin nightdress, taut as a round drum. And underneath, the child poking as if in a morning stretch.

Petronela lovingly stroked the muslin package. "This dress means the kingdom to me, and only you can keep it safe. Find Esmerelda, and leave this land," she commanded as she shoved the package into Nadzia's arms. Next, she pulled something from her pocket. "Thank you for lending me your necklace for the ball. It was a perfect match. But you must wear it now and always. It will be our sign."

Nadzia touched the amber pendant as the queen clasped it around her neck. Her mother's necklace. It felt right to have it back again. The faint scent of old pine forest wafted up as the amber warmed to her skin. No other necklace emitted a scent such as this. It reminded her of home. Of safety.

"Tell no one where you are going. Esmerelda has bound us together, and we will find each other. If not me, my daughter. It is her legacy. Do this for me, I beg you."

"Of course. But promise me you'll follow me if you can. You shouldn't stay here either."

"I stay by Marek. We'll be fine."

Heart racing, Nadzia ran out of the room, down the secret staircase and on through a hidden corridor. If Nela thought everything would be fine, she wouldn't have sent Nadzia away.

Oh, what is happening?

She battled her emotions as she tried to maintain a clear head. She expected to serve the queen until her old age, like Esmerelda. To maybe be nursemaid to the little ones. Now what was she to do? She'd played at espionage before and she wasn't good at it. Run and hide. It was all she could think.

The air chilled Nadzia to her core as she ran down a dark passageway into the deepest part of the castle. A single torch on each wall cast a pale, flickering light on the uneven damp stones. She crushed the muslin-wrapped bundle in her arms, but she daren't let go her grip. Tears threatened to spill out of her tired eyes. Was it only last night they had held the annual ball? Today the world was upside down.

Petronela should have allowed her to stay until the baby was born. The child would have been like a little brother or sister she never had. All these months helping the queen prepare—knitting the soft blankets and sewing the tiny clothes and the little nappies. Now someone else would help Nela care for the wee one.

She choked back her emotions. There would be time for self-pity once she made it to the mountains. Back to Esmerelda. At least if the queen had to send her away, she was sending her back to the only mother she had ever known.

She paused at a junction where the passage split in two. It was to confuse and divide any attacking army that made it this far into the castle. After a slight hesitation, she chose left.

"Nadzia!" Her name echoed against the walls.

She stopped. Hope rose. "My queen?" Nadzia retraced her steps. Had Nela changed her mind?

Several corners later, she found the young queen braced against the wall breathing heavily and holding her rounded stomach.

"Is it time?" Nadzia rushed forward and knelt, hands reaching up to feel the baby elbowing its cramped space.

"No. I'm just out of breath. I forgot to give you something."

Nadzia squinted in the dim light. Dangling from the queen's other hand were her shoes. *The* shoes.

"Those, too?" she squeaked.

"One. You must, so you can find me again."

Only if I'm desperate. I'll not risk someone learning of their power.

CHAPTER 32

*N*adzia used her secret key to open the door. It worked silently and smoothly, as she would expect from Esmerelda's handiwork. This back way out of the castle was known only to the royal family and their most trusted servants. When she emerged, all was quiet amidst the firs on the side of the mountain. It was like stepping out into another world, going from the man-made splendor of the castle to untouched wilderness and all its created beauty. She paused for only a moment to get her bearings. Then she raced down the valley and then up the mountain toward Esmerelda's place.

Not used to the exercise anymore, her lungs were on fire, her legs sluggish.

She was surprised Esmerelda hadn't warned them what was coming. With her cottage so close to the border, she would have known if an army crossed the pass. But when Nadzia entered their little valley, there was no smoke rising from the chimney, and the animals were silent. Had Esmerelda overslept? She did like her tea in bed, but by now the animals would be trying to wake her up. Nadzia wasn't worried that the soldiers had harmed her. Esmerelda had her own ways of staying out of sight.

Nadzia knocked before trying the handle. At no response, she opened the unlocked door and rushed in. "Esmerelda, terrible news…"

The shuttered windows blocked the light, but even in the dimness, she could see the place was deserted. There was no life inside.

"Esmerelda?" She faltered. It had been some time since Nadzia had visited, but surely Esmerelda would have come to the castle to say goodbye?

Nadzia scoured the place looking for any indication of where Esmerelda could have gone. Was it a short trip, or something more permanent? The answer lay on the sideboard, which was empty of everything save Esmerelda's favorite tatting shuttle, one carved by Janosik. Nadzia picked it up, feeling the worn spot where Esmerelda's thumb would rest. Esmerelda had talked about needing to move on to help other girls, and now she had. This was her parting gift.

Nadzia blinked rapidly, pocketing the shuttle. The skills Esmerelda taught her would help her make a living no matter where she went. And where should she go? Rome came to mind. Maybe a small town outside the city would suffice until she could reestablish contact with Petronela.

Quickly, she packed a bag of things she would need from the pantry, which Esmerelda had left fully stocked. Maybe the fairy godmother had known what was coming and knew Nadzia would go to the cottage first before going anywhere else.

She'd have to get away on her own while the focus was still on the castle. Once Petronela's stepsisters realized the dress was gone, it wouldn't take them long to figure out where it had gone.

She paused at the doorway to say goodbye, but a noise from behind got her moving again. The army was crossing the mountain path. She could hear them already, which meant they were a large force. She fled to the safety of the forest.

But as the noise grew louder, she grew curious about just how many were coming. She stopped and hid her sacks at the base of a thicket before climbing a sturdy tree. There they were, a steady line of warriors coming down from the pass.

Marek, distracted by the death of his father and the pregnancy of his new bride, hadn't noticed the signs. Or maybe his spies hadn't done their jobs to warn him. Whatever the reason, it didn't matter now. The army was coming and with a force unlike she'd ever seen. If the dress and the shoes were as dear to Nela as she said, it was right for her to send Nadzia away to keep them safe. For the time being, no one would be interested in a lone mountain girl. All attention would be on the fight for the castle, for the kingdom.

While she had the advantage of adrenaline and fear spurring her on, she climbed back down and kept up a steady pace through the trees. She nibbled on cheese and biscuits she'd slipped into her sack. Later, there would be the dried sausage. After that, Nadzia hoped for the kindness of strangers.

CHAPTER 33

*I*t was a long, arduous trip, but she made it to Italy. By the end of her journey everyone called her the gypsy woman, and she felt like one. Wearing clothes that hid her shape and hats with wide brims that hid her face, she traveled incognito until she felt safe.

She did odd jobs when she could to help pay for a ride on the back of a wagon. If she was riding, her feet got to rest, and she had the time to work on her lace. By the time she walked into Rome she had a good stockpile of dainty lace to sell and had learned enough of the language to survive.

Eager for news of what was happening back home, she loitered in all the areas travelers would cross and took up conversation with anyone who had an accent similar to the one she had purposely lost.

One woman who eyed all her wares but didn't buy told her a king had died "somewhere up there."

Then later, a young couple who bought lace to adorn their newborn's christening dress said it wasn't a king who died, but a queen.

And a third traveler said neither had died but they were under arrest, not able to leave the castle.

"And the baby?" she pressed this third traveler, as his information was the most hopeful. "Was there a baby?"

"Don't know anything about an infant."

"Thank you." Nadzia was grateful for any snippet she could glean. She handed him a small lace bookmark in the shape of a cross. "For the lady in your life."

Eventually, she couldn't stand not knowing any longer. It had been months. Was it safe for her to return or not?

Nadzia carefully crafted a letter, leaving out all information as to her whereabouts, and only just enough of a hint of her identity that Petronela would know it was from her. With a breathy prayer, she sent the letter and waited.

The reply came six months later and not in the form she expected. She was renting a room from a sweet elderly woman who needed help around the house. The house was on the outskirts of the city, in an oft-overlooked area where Nadzia was never bothered. She was on the lane returning from market when she witnessed a Burgosov representative come knocking at the door.

Instantly, she was on guard, guessing who the man was by his accent as he spoke to her landlady. The accents from both kingdoms were similar but noticeably different to native speakers.

Nadzia had never used her address in the letter she sent. This man had somehow tracked her down anyway. Ears straining, Nadzia continued walking past the house, listening closely and praying her landlady wouldn't see her and call her out.

Stolen. Runaway. Servant.

Those were the only words she needed to hear. As soon as she was out of their line of sight she began to run. A law-abiding woman, if the widow believed him, she would tell him all she knew of her quiet boarder.

Nadzia couldn't go back to the little house. Not now. Not ever. Her collection of books on her bedside table and her pile of lace would have to be payment enough to the woman to tide her over until she found another boarder. All Nadzia needed was her hidden package and Esmerelda's shuttle, which she kept on her person at all times.

All was not well at the castle. Her time was not yet.

Realizing how wise it was for her to keep the dress and diamond shoe hidden in another location, she raced there now, a hollow tree trunk that had fallen down a steep ravine. It was difficult to get to and so unlikely anyone would ever stumble across the bundles hidden deep inside.

After retrieving the precious items, Nadzia fled the town. She traveled relentlessly through the night. At the first sound of a traveler on the same road, she hid. Feeling scared and alone, she tried to calm her mind to form a plan. She may never be able to return home again. What did that mean for Petronela? For Esmerelda's magical creations?

CHAPTER 34

*A*nother six months later, Nadzia tried again. And again, a castle guard came looking for her.

A year later. Same thing.

Another year. Same.

Until one year something different happened.

A guard came, and he not only spoke with the accent of home, but the first thing he said was that he was looking for mother Esmerelda and her daughter, Nadzia.

Nadzia, who never gave out her true name, was returning from her morning walk and hid behind the neighbor's bushes. The quiet lane only had a few houses, and only one that took boarders. He would have learned that in town.

The woman who owned the house said she knew of no one by that name, and that her current boarder was a quiet young girl.

He thanked the woman and left.

Nadzia waited for him to get a little bit ahead, then followed him. He walked to the local pub, and as she watched through the window, he found a table in a quiet corner.

She knew the cook—taught her to make the most delicious stew—and so snuck in through the kitchen. They were gearing up for the dinner rush as evidenced by all the soup pots filled to the top while the aroma of garlic and leek and bacon filled the air.

"Marguerite," said the cook when she saw Nadzia. "When are you going to marry my brother? I want you as my sister-in-law." The family-run business was staffed by mother, father, brother, and two sisters.

Nadzia laughed. "You would make a wonderful sister-in-law. But I don't think your brother and I are suited." The brother in question was a flirtatious thing in no mind to settle down anytime soon. Nor would Nadzia live in this place long enough to prove how ill-suited they would be. This cook was the first real friend she'd had since leaving home. Moving away every six months to a year made a girl not bother with deep friendships.

"May I play waitress on the corner table?" she asked.

The cook looked through the open window into the dining area.

"Young. Handsome, dark looks." She spun around and placed a hand on her hip. "That's your type?"

Nadzia shrugged. *May as well let the cook think so.*

The cook tossed a dish towel at her. "Fine. But remember to give him his bill. My brother always lets the pretty girls eat our soup for free."

"Thanks." Nadzia grabbed a tray to look official.

The suspected guard had kept his eye on the front door. He calmly sipped coffee like he was a local and sat here every day. Her friend was correct. He was handsome. Strong, with the cut features of the highlanders. Just looking at him made her homesick.

"Anything else I can get you?" she asked him.

He glanced at her, and then waved his hand. "A refill later."

"Are you waiting for someone?"

"Perhaps."

"I've heard that accent before, are you from the Tatras?"

He adjusted his position away from her. An indicator that he was uncomfortable.

"Thereabouts," he said.

"Any more trouble in the area?"

"No more so than usual. Everyone has adjusted to the new regime." He took a sip. "For now."

"What ever happened to the young king and queen? I heard they'd barely come to power when they were invaded."

He turned toward her, leaning forward on the table. "You've got a lot of questions for a serving girl."

She raised her eyebrows and shrugged like she didn't care. "I gather news. Helps with the tips when I can pass on information."

"This is old information. What is your interest in the royal family?"

Uh oh. She was getting too straightforward with her line of questioning.

"What happened to them is a mystery, so people still talk. Ready for your refill now?"

He handed her his cup.

She rushed back into the kitchen and leaned on a cutting table to catch her breath.

"Wow, he's got you flustered," said the cook as she spooned out her famous leek soup. "Never thought I'd see the day you blushed over a man."

Nadzia held her hands to her cheeks. She wasn't a scared young girl anymore. Time had passed and she'd grown up. Besides, he called them the royal family, which might indicate his allegiance. She would take a risk and tell the man who she was, in this public place, and see what happened. Even if he'd come for the magical items, he wouldn't find them.

Nadzia stood upright and collected her nerves. "If it looks like I'm in trouble, would you send your brother in to help? I may need to leave town quickly."

The cook set down the bowl. "You're scaring me. Is he someone you've been running from?"

"The opposite. I've been running for so long, and he might be someone I can run to." Nadzia didn't want to get her hopes up, but ever since she'd left the castle, this was the first sign of hope she'd had.

"Be smart about it. I'll be watching," the cook said.

CHAPTER 35

*N*adzia poured another coffee, and with an encouraging nod from the cook, used her hip to bump open the door.

"Here you are." She plunked down the cup, spilling a little because of her jittery nerves. "Oops, I'll get that." She wiped the table and casually asked, "So, have you got a name?"

"Aron. And you are?"

She hesitated. To tell or not to tell? She glanced back at the kitchen and saw the cook watching, biting her lip. How much longer could Nadzia keep running and not know what she was running from? She was tired of this transient life.

"I'm Nadzia."

The man's eyes opened wide. They were a beautiful rich brown with gold flecks. Then he smiled a relieved smile. "They told me you'd be clever."

"Who did?"

He lowered his voice. "Marek and Nela."

"May I?" she indicated the chair across from him.

"Please."

"Do you have news for me? It's been so long."

"Our land is remote and not many pass through it anymore. The new rulers have cut us off from the rest of the world."

"You talked with Marek and Nela?"

"Let me start with a letter I intercepted addressed for the queen. I happened to be on hand the day it came in and it fell out of the mailbag, right at my feet, almost as if by magic."

Nadzia suppressed a smile. She wondered if Esmerelda was back in the area.

"I sneaked it in to Nela, and it was like I was giving her the kingdom back."

Now Nadzia couldn't hold back a smile. Her friend was alive and they'd made contact.

"I want to know everything, all at once," she said. "Everyone is well? The baby?"

"The baby is a bright, curious little girl now. The Burgosovs banished the family to a cottage up in the mountains, but they say they are happy."

Esmerelda's cottage?

"And the kingdom? What has happened?"

He shook his head. "It's weak. It will not end well for our people, at least not in the near future. The Burgosovs only half-heartedly protect the town and promote trade."

"What should we do?"

He looked surprised. "Nothing. It's over. The Burgosovs dismissed the army; imprisoned the leaders. We have no fighting force to take the kingdom back."

"But the townspeople?"

"Overall, they're fine. There's no more fighting, so they are content, or at least at peace with the way things are right now. The Burgosovs aren't cruel, necessarily, but they do favor the land across the mountain.

She tapped her fingers on the table. After all these years, this news felt like a letdown. A storybook ending that didn't happen. She realized now, she'd expected a call to action. Had been waiting for a revolt to turn the tide again so that she could go home.

"You look lost. What did I say?"

"Nothing. Tell me more about Nela. Is she calling me home?" She asked even though she suspected the answer was not what she wanted.

He leaned back in his chair. "I think I have disappointing news for you."

"She doesn't want me to return."

"On the contrary. She does, but says it would be best for you to stay where you are, if where you are is a good place." His gaze took in the small dining area, the regulars eating up at the bar, the curious waitresses keeping an eye on Aron and Nadzia. "Is this a good place?"

"It is, except now you know where I am." She couldn't help but feel abandoned. If Nela and her family were now living away from the castle, why shouldn't she be reunited with them?

"Does it matter that I know about you?"

She shrugged. "I don't know what matters anymore." And what about the dress and diamond shoe? What was she supposed to do with those?

"I can't leave you like this. Let me treat you to dinner before I go. Where is the best place in town?"

"You're already here. No better food anywhere."

"Great. Then when your shift is over, will you join me?"

She grinned. "I don't work here. I just needed to be sure of you."

He laughed, a hearty sound that reminded her of tall mountains and deep valleys all at once. Home. And he spent the rest of the evening telling her all about home. How he'd worked for Nela's family since he was old enough to feed the chickens and that was where his loyalty came in. He was funny and sweet, and Nadzia was sad to see the waitresses putting up chairs so they could sweep the floors at the end of the night.

"I didn't realize it was so late," he said. "But I'm glad to see a smile on your face now."

"You've been wonderful company. I feel closer to home than I have in years."

"One last thing I neglected to mention earlier," he said. "Nela said you were to keep what she gave you until her daughter comes for it."

CHAPTER 36

That night, Nadzia lay awake for hours going over and over everything she had learned. Nela didn't want her to return to the mountains, yet still wanted her to keep Esmerelda's gifts for her. It was a dangerous assignment, but one she would do gladly as it honored both her friend and the one she thought of as her mother.

Giving up on sleep, she tossed the covers aside. A spot of tea might do the trick. She padded down to the kitchen and as she readied the kettle, a glimmer in the garden caught her eye. Esmerelda!

Nadzia flew out the door, and then down the moonlit porch steps. The dewy grass was cold and wet on her bare feet.

"Esmerelda!" Nadzia threw herself at her mother. "I came back to the cottage and you were gone."

"You didn't need me anymore."

"But we did. The castle was attacked and the queen sent me away with your gifts to her. She wants them kept safe. But now that you're here we can go back. We can help them." Nadzia pulled away, anxious to get going.

"I'm afraid not." Esmerelda held Nadzia's hands. "Their

kingdom has toppled and will not rise again. The land is destined to belong to the people, but it will be fought over for years to come."

Why was everyone telling her there was nothing to be done? "I don't understand."

"Are you happy to stay connected to the queen, who is no longer a queen?"

"Of course. Does she need me? The child? I can leave right now."

Esmerelda took her arm and walked her to the wicker chairs on the porch. Nadzia chose instead to sit on the porch swing. She needed to keep moving, if only to pump the swing with her toe against the wood planks.

"She and Marek and the young girl are fine. The girl is a delight, and they are happy they have each other." Her face grew serious. "But it is still dangerous for you. They still look for you."

"But I'm no one. A simple mountain girl," she said, exasperated.

"You know what makes you dangerous. The Burgosovs are still looking for the dress and shoes. They are terribly vindictive, and think they have a claim on them as part of the royal treasury, among other reasons. It is also for your sake that Nela wants you to stay away."

"You've talked to her?"

Esmerelda retrieved a package from behind the chair. "Nela sends her peasant dress and her wedding gown. She would like you to keep watch over all three. She feels like they need to be together to preserve her story." She handed the bundle to Nadzia. "And the other shoe. It's been in peril several times."

"I don't understand." Nadzia opened a corner of the package to reveal the glittery bodice. She would be happy to be Nela's keeper of the wardrobe—back home.

"I bound you and Petronela together, thinking you would

remain in the castle. Since this is not so, I wanted to make sure both of you are willing to continue the arrangement."

"Yes, but how?"

"You've met Aron?"

"Last night."

"He can be your go-between. He is known and well-liked in the castle."

"They are not suspicious? He worked for Nela's family for years."

"No one paid him any attention other than Nela. And in his new profession, they don't recognize him."

Nadzia raised her eyebrows. "He's quite unforgettable. Did you notice how pretty his eyes are?"

"I hadn't." Esmerelda gave a knowing look.

"Pretty eyes won't do me any good if they have to go back to the castle."

"Hush, don't talk so loud, he's right over there."

"What?" Embarrassed, Nadzia peered into the lilac bushes where Esmerelda had indicated.

"I brought him with me. Thought it would be faster this way to work out the details. Aron, join us, please," Esmerelda said.

"With pleasure."

Nadzia wilted. How much of the conversation had he heard?

Grinning, he sat close beside her on the bench.

Apparently, a lot of the conversation. He stared at her with a goofy grin on his face and she couldn't help but grin back.

He appeared practical, honorable, and faithful. If both Petronela and Esmerelda thought him worthy, then she could trust him.

"Something for you to consider," Aron said before clearing his throat. "I've been listening to Petronela's stories about you for years. After our long talk, I know you are exactly as she described you…and more."

Petronela held her breath. *Where is he going with this?*

He shifted closer, his hands clasped. "I think we'll work well together. As a tailor, I have an excuse to come here to buy expensive fabrics and lace for the royal household. You sell lace?"

"Yes." *Lace? That is all he wants?*

"And, if you would consider me." He cleared his throat again, looking at his hands.

"Yes?"

"If you would consider me a friend. A good friend..."

Nadzia nodded. "A trusted friend."

"Yes."

Aron met her gaze, and Nadzia's heart raced.

"I'll leave you two to work out the details," Esmerelda said as she stood.

Nadzia stood with her. "Wait. You just got here. Couldn't you stay a few days? A week or two?"

"Walk with me," Esmerelda said.

They left the yard and found a dirt path on the edge of a meadow. Bright white daisies dotted the field and shone in the moonlight. While they walked, Nadzia spoke of as many reasons she could think of that Esmerelda should stay with her. Or nearby, if she preferred.

Esmerelda ignored them all, instead saying, "I found out who your mother was."

Nadzia froze. After all these years? For a passing moment she didn't want to hear who it was. After being on the run all this time and finally making a connection back home. Seeing Esmerelda again. Considering a future with Aron. It was all too much. She searched Esmerelda's eyes. "She picked you for a reason. You are my mother."

Esmerelda let out a sigh, and Nadzia realized how concerned the woman had been about delivering the news.

"You didn't mind your growing up years with me?" Esmerelda asked.

"Mind? I loved them. Of all the childhoods, I think mine was the best." She put her arm around Esmerelda's shoulders, wanting to convey just how contented her growing-up years had been.

"Do you want to know who she was? She's someone you came in close association with, but never actually met."

Was. Past tense. "Did she know about me?"

"I imagine she had ways to learn about you without any of us suspecting. Possibly through Janosik's wandering tales."

Nadzia's mind raced thinking of possibilities but coming up empty. "Who is she?"

"I'm sorry to say she has passed now. She came from over the mountain. The aunt of a certain maid in the Burgosov household. I believe she was dying when you went to rescue Petronela."

If only she'd known then. It would have been her last chance to meet her mother. Ask about where she came from. What her family was like.

"Then the maid who took the diamond was a cousin." She wondered where that maid was now. Did she move into the castle with the Burgosovs?

"I'll find out more for you, if I can. Janosik can help."

"Thank you for telling me. I thought I had stopped wondering, but I hadn't." She offered a bewildered smile.

Esmerelda gave her an uncharacteristic hug before she turned practical again. "Speaking of diamonds. You have permission to use the heart stones as needed. Marek and Petronela have been quite clever in the ways they've been quietly helping their kingdom. Keep in mind, it should be rarely, and never sell them in the same town so that people do not grow suspicious."

"Of course."

"When I do something, I do it well." She nodded toward Aron. "Now, off you go, Nadzia. It's time for me to go on my way again."

With one last hug, Nadzia left Esmerelda again, to go toward another, uncertain future. But one which she anticipated would be filled with love and adventure.

*T*he princess glanced over her shoulder as she knocked on the small door at the back of the townhouse. The front of the building was a plain shop with a swinging wooden sign that simply read "Tailor." She hoped that at long last she had found the right shop.

A small light in the window at the neighbor's house cast too much light for the princess to be comfortable. No one must see her here. She stepped back into the shadows, trying to blend in with the ivy climbing the brick wall.

The door upon which she had knocked creaked open a tiny crack, exposing the landing to a strip of light. The princess leaned forward. "Esmerelda wishes it," she whispered.

There was a small cry and an ancient woman with deep-set eyes pulled her inside. The woman locked and then bolted the door behind them.

She doused all the lights. Her bony hands squeezed the princess's shoulders. "Who are you?" she asked. Her voice was quiet and raspy, like dry autumn leaves scraping against the ground when blown by the wind.

The princess did not know if it was safe to reveal her identity.

"My engagement ball is in three days. I've come for my grandmother's dress."

The old woman's hands found their way to the princess's face. They shook as the old woman felt the princess's features. "Her granddaughter?" the woman rasped. "But why not my queen? Why has she not come?" There was disappointment in the old voice.

The princess swallowed. "My grandmother has gone to her eternal reward. She told me how to find you when the time came. She wanted me to wear her dress."

A suppressed choking sound came from the woman. There was shuffling, then a *shick* of a match strike. A candle was lit and the light began to bob away from the entrance. The princess quickly followed.

The old woman led the way down a long hallway. She took a key from around her neck and opened a door to a narrow staircase that went sharply downward. The princess reached out to help, but the woman brushed her away. "I'm not dead yet," she snapped. The princess saw tears on the old woman's wrinkled face before she turned and led the way down the stairs.

"I'm sorry to be the one to tell you about Grandmother," the princess said gently.

"The last time I saw your grandmother was when she told me to leave the castle," said the old woman over her shoulder. "Since that sorry day we have corresponded by letter." The woman paused to catch her breath. "I hoped to see her one last time on this earth."

She hung her head and continued down the stairs, holding the candle in front. "T'was not meant to be."

The air grew cooler with each step and the musty smell of mildew hung heavy in the air. The princess wondered at the state of the dress in this terrible place. Would it be moth-eaten and moldy? This woman should have found a better hiding place for the dress. The princess began to think of other options. Could she get a new dress made in such a short amount of time? Was her trip here a waste of time?

At the bottom of the stairs stood another locked door. The woman reached over her head to a shelf and pulled down a key. She opened the door and then handed the candle to the princess. The door opened to a small closet. As the door swung open, the princess saw the closet was no ordinary wardrobe. The door was a foot thick. Sweet-smelling air whooshed out. On the bottom shelf was a single wooden steamer trunk with leather straps and an eagle crest.

Another key and the trunk was opened.

The princess tried to look inside the trunk but the woman's back blocked her view. The woman closed the lid and turned towards the princess. In her arms she held a large, cloth-wrapped package.

The princess then looked down at the tips of her pretty traveling boots. "And the shoes?"

"It's all there." The woman stiffened as if offended. "I had this special closet built. I suggest you do the same. If you have a moment, I can get you the name of the man who constructs these cabinets."

"Oh," said the princess, startled. "Grandmother's instructions were to return the dress and shoes to you as soon as I could."

The old woman's mouth twitched into a smile then settled back to a straight line. "I see."

"There are three of us, sisters, and we are each consumed with the dress. Grandmother says none of us may possess it. We are also to ensure you and your family have no need the rest of your life." She looked sheepish. "Do you have kin? You are almost as old as Grandmother was. If we need to make other arrangements…"

The old woman's smile flickered once more. "I've had years to plan procedures for such a time as this."

From her pocket she pulled a card. She still held the bundle.

She tucked the card into a fold in the wrapping. "Blessings on your wedding, child." She finally handed the bundle to the princess.

"Go out this way." The old woman took the candle and then led the way to a half door at the back of the room. "It will be dark. Keep your right hand on the wall. You will make two turns, then go up a slope. You will be able to find your way home from there."

Impulsively, the princess hugged the old woman. She felt a thin, bony frame underneath the plain clothing. "Thank you."

The woman hugged her back with surprising strength. "God go with you."

AUTHOR'S NOTE

If you enjoyed reading the Cinderella books in the Fairy-tale Inheritance series, be sure to leave a review to help other readers decide if this is the book series for them. *Cinderella's Dress* and *Cinderella's Shoes* were originally published by a traditional publisher, but now are being published exclusively by the author who relies on word of mouth advertising.

To learn more about the Fairy-tale Inheritance Series, check out Shonna Slayton's website You'll find articles and photos related to the books. You can also download a free fairy tale when you sign up to receive email updates on the new books.

ShonnaSlayton.com

ACKNOWLEDGMENTS

Many thanks to critique partners Kristi Doyle and Sarah Chanis for their sage advice and input during early (and subsequent) drafts. Lisa Knapp, proofreader extraordinaire, provided the final polish. A special shout out goes to my steady beta readers Andrea Huelsenbeck and Rebekah Slayton who continue to give me feedback and encouragement to keep me going. I'm also grateful for two newsletter subscribers who were willing to roll up their sleeves and double as beta readers: LynnDell Watson and Alicia Laxton. I hope I didn't miss anyone as I sent out a few ARCs but they didn't all make it back to my inbox for feedback. (Also, my brain is somewhat spacey at this stage of the game.) And last, but certainly not least...cover artist Jenny Zemanek made this beautiful cover for the novella so it would match the style of the Fairy-tale Inheritance Series.

Printed in Great Britain
by Amazon

69567294R00121